T0017913

"At once tender and cruel, insolent and profound, Malika Moustadraf is an exceptional and courageous short story writer who confronts the harshest realities of her country, Morocco. Her characters, with all their humor and complexity, will stay with you for a long time."

—**Leïla Slimani**, author of *In the Country of Others*

"Malika Moustadraf's short stories, elegantly translated in Alice Guthrie's raw prose, draw the reader into tender inner lives—from a breastfeeding mother flirting on the internet, to a gender nonconforming sex worker, to a young man grappling with desire itself. The writing here is taut, the juxtapositions unexpected, the observations unflinching. Moustadraf's voice guides the reader into full-blooded worlds of humor and disharmony."

—**Selma Dabbagh**, author of *Out of It*

"*Blood Feast* is a dark, edgy, and compelling collection from an author who should be celebrated internationally. Malika Moustadraf is a master at describing the hidden desires, lurking ferocity, sharp beauty, and glinting pain of her characters, so many of whom toil and fight unseen and unheard by wider society. In these gritty (and witty) stories, the complexity of today's world is brought into clear focus, with all its savagery and all its contingent saving graces. Moustadraf's world is one of survivors and pugilists, strivers and grifters, dreamers and hustlers all hungry to be somewhere or something or someone else. The author writes their lives with poignancy and poetic grace."

—**Bidisha**, author of *The Future of Serious Art*

"Haunting, caustic, and unflinching, this hypnotizing collection of stories is like being gifted a secret box of dark, complex chocolates."

—**Saleem Haddad**, author of *Guapa*

BLOOD FEAST

The Complete Short Stories of
MALIKA MOUSTADRAF

Translated from the Arabic by
ALICE GUTHRIE

THE FEMINIST PRESS
AT THE CITY UNIVERSITY OF NEW YORK
NEW YORK CITY

Published in 2022 by the Feminist Press
at the City University of New York
The Graduate Center
365 Fifth Avenue, Suite 5406
New York, NY 10016

feministpress.org

First Feminist Press edition 2022

The short story collection *Trente-Six* was published in Arabic by the Moroccan Short Story Research Group in Casablanca in 2004. The last four stories in this book were published in the Moroccan literary magazine *QS* in 2006 and 2007.

  This book was made possible thanks to a grant from the New York State Council on the Arts with the support of the Governor and the New York State Legislature.

This book is supported in part by an award from the National ART WORKS. Endowment for the Arts.

First printing February 2022

Cover design by Sukruti Anah Staneley
Text design by Drew Stevens

Library of Congress Cataloging-in-Publication Data is available for this title.

PRINTED IN THE UNITED STATES OF AMERICA

Issam,
I see you as a wonderful homeland I would like
to belong to.

Abdellatif,
I know you have a huge heart inside of you,
and not a heavy boulder.

CONTENTS

THE RUSE

Shaibia raised her scrawny brown hand to her upper lip, preparing to let out a celebratory ululation. Her sister Hada stopped her. "Don't trill! You want everyone in the whole karian to come join us?"

"But it's such a happy day!"

"I'm scared of the evil eye of envy on you. When the neighbors find out about your daughter's betrothal, they might do a number on you to mess up the marriage."

"You're right. I won't tell anybody anything until the last minute, especially Aïcha the Slaughtered. You know she's got a unibrow."

"I know . . . Anyway, you can't imagine how happy I am that Fatima's finally getting married! Who's the groom?"

"Someone who works in Italy, so she'll live in a

real house, made of cement, that the sunlight shines into."

Shaibia sighed, then went on, "She'll finally be free of this shack and all its problems. No more standing in line to fetch water, no more doing you-know-what out in the open."

Hada took a little disapproving sip of her tea.

"Really? So she'll live with her in-laws, and her husband will be far away from her all year; he won't come visit more than once a year—"

Shaibia cut in. "It doesn't matter. What does she want with a man suffocating her all year long?"

"Well anyway, your daughter is a good girl, she's respectful and obedient and she deserves the best. She always goes straight to that factory, and after work she comes straight home again. She does you proud."

Shaibia went quiet. She scratched her head through her colorful scarf for a little while, as if pondering a critical issue. Then suddenly she said, "For the jihaaz they have to buy two of everything— her jihaaz has to be so lavish that we can blind

Dawia the doughnut-maker's wife and Kalthoum, even Kharboush the hash-seller's wife."

"Definitely, seeing as barely any bride-price will be paid. So on top of buying her a wedding ring he'll have to get her a bracelet or a necklace, plus—"

Shaibia hushed her with a wave of the hand, drew in closer, and lowered her voice to say, "Listen, I'm going to take my daughter to the doctor."

Hada slapped her palm to her chest in shock.

"Why? Is she sick?"

"No . . . I need to get a certificate that proves her virginity."

Hada gasped.

"You doubt your own daughter?"

"No, not at all. My daughter, may Allah be content with her, she's not like some other girls are these days: she doesn't get led astray. She keeps herself to herself, bless her. But do you remember what happened to Aïcha the Slaughtered's daughter last summer?"

"Of course I remember—who could forget? It was the scandal to end all scandals! When the groom went to deflower the bride, he was back out half an hour later cursing and swearing and saying that the goods were damaged, the girl wasn't a virgin. Her mother claimed it was the groom's problem, that he was unable to carry out his assignment because he'd overdone the weed and booze, as well as being the victim of a thiqaaf curse. That was how the wedding flipped into a funeral—so much shouting and fistfighting, then it degenerated into a battle with batons! And the bridal couple ended up at the police station. And then that poor girl was divorced and she hasn't known peace for a single day since."

"That's why I want to get a virginity certificate and give it to the groom's family, so that we avoid any problems."

"You're so right. Let me take her for you. We can go tomorrow, don't worry."

Shaibia began smacking her thighs with her open palms.

"Woe is me, what are you saying . . . I can't believe my daughter isn't a virgin! How did this happen? And when? She doesn't go out, except to the factory, and she always comes home exactly on time; she never spends the night away from home, ever! This has got to be a mistake. The doctor must have messed up. I don't trust women doctors; they don't know what they're doing. I'll take her tomorrow— no, I'm taking her today!—to see a male doctor."

"Calm yourself, my sister, the doctor didn't mess up. Your daughter confessed to me."

For a moment Shaibia was like a wax figure, apparently unable to process what Hada had just told her. Then, catching up, she said, "Confessed what?"

Hada summoned all her strength, steeling herself to throw the second grenade in her sister's face.

"She . . . she doesn't work at the factory. She's a regular at one of the brothels, in fact, and . . ."

Shaibia collapsed instantly onto the reed mat at their feet, thrown into an attack of violent sobbing.

Then, just as suddenly, she wiped her eyes and got back up on her feet to declare, "I don't ever want to see her face again. She's to leave my house right now."

Trying to console her, Hada took her hand.

"Well, as they saying goes, 'If the meat smells bad, its owners are responsible.' And to every problem there's a solution."

"Except this one. There's no solution to this problem! This was a dream deal, and it's gone down the drain. No cement house, no jihaaz, no wedding, and what am I supposed to tell the groom? 'Sorry, we changed our minds'?"

"You won't tell him anything, because everything's going to work out and happen just like we planned it."

"How?!"

Hada was silent for a moment, drawing a deep breath. She mopped her brow. Then, with a cunning look on her face, she said, "I'll take her to a doctor to get her hymen replaced."

"Replace her virginity? Is that possible?"

"Of course it's possible."

"But no doctor would ever agree to do that."

"That's what you think . . . I know a doctor in the building where I work, in Maârif. There's not one single forbidden procedure he won't perform. From abortions to hymen restoration, and who knows what other even more shocking things he does in secret too."

In a voice quavering with terrified hope, Shaibia asked her sister, "And how much does he charge?"

"I don't know . . . I'll find out. Don't be scared."

"But won't the groom be able to tell? Won't he have doubts?"

"No, no, you can rest assured, your daughter'll be like new."

Shaibia heaved a tentative sigh of relief.

"The wedding is truly magnificent," said Aïcha the Slaughtered. "May the bride be very happy!"

"Yes, the groom bought two of everything, as well as a huge bracelet and a ring," Hada told her.

"Our girls will be next, inshallah," said Dawia with a sigh.

Shaibia's face was wan, and she kept putting her hand over her heart. Hada pinched her.

"Smile, or people will suspect a scandal."

After a while a long ululation rang out, and the mother of the groom emerged with a brass tray. On it was a pair of white sirwal underwear spotted with blood. Hada took the tray and bore it aloft, over her head, and began to sing:

"Blood on my head, brothers,
    and not made in no lab!
Blood on the cloth, sisters,
    and not off no butcher's slab!"

DELUSION

He left the house cursing everything at the top of his lungs—from the two elderly people who had brought him into this rotten world to his sister, who had married a Frenchman, gone off with him to his country, and hadn't kept her promise. He remembered what she'd said at the airport: "I only married this Christian for your sakes. One month, and you'll all have the paperwork you need to join me over there. Don't worry!"

He had believed her. And then a month had passed, dragging other miserable, boring months along after it, all nauseatingly similar, and she hadn't kept her promise. He was tired of seeing his mother come home at the end of the day with her employers' leftover food and hand-me-downs. He was tired of his father smoking so much weed that all he could

9

do was languish in the corner of the room, about as good company as a scarecrow. And he was even more tired of standing at the end of the road with his crate of cigarette boxes set out in front of him, selling loosies. He smoked more than he sold. He would watch passersby and sit with Hamu, who watched over people's parked cars for money, and tell him anything and everything about the neighbors, and about people he knew or didn't know. He would hit on the scantily clad girls passing by, and they'd look at him in total revulsion, as if he were some disgusting piece of food long past its expiration date. A real top-grade singer's voice belted out from the radio, with a half-brayed, half-snorted public declaration of how horny and frustrated she was: *Hug him, squeeze him, kiss him . . .*

Hearing this ignited something in him, sparked a great hunger for all sorts of things, and he sensed that old beast Desire, lying dormant somewhere in his body, let out a ravenous, cruel howl. His eyes drilled into the plump buttocks passing by: the way they heaved and rolled was so indecent, so thrilling, and so terrifying. Whichever way he turned he found bulging breasts pointing directly at the thing underneath his belly, provoking it, grinding on his nerves brutally, ferociously, without mercy. He concentrated on sipping his black coffee, so as not to do anything crazy he might come to regret later. Even the imam at the local mosque had been caught a few times by the young men from the neighborhood sneaking a look at the girls and fumbling with that thing under his paunch, his ancient prayer beads creaking between his fingers. *You've got an excuse, our imam—if Eve got Adam thrown out of Eden, then she's bound to make you succumb to earthly pleasures, isn't she?*

He looked over at Hamu and said irritably, "What they're subjecting us to is violence, that's what it is. One day I'll make a placard saying 'No to violence against men,' and I'll march around the streets with it. And they wonder why rapes happen? The world is full of slu—" He hawked up some phlegm. "Those girls are the lucky ones in this country. They can't even tell the difference between a book and a billy club—but all they have to do is show a bit of thigh, put on some makeup, and every single closed door swings open for them! And you and I know all about closed doors, don't we?"

He would fill with rage when he saw the neighborhood girls: no older than twenty, and each with her own cell phone. Some of them had even bought themselves cars and now wanted to buy apartments instead of hellholes like the one he lived in, disingenuously called a "house."

When his sister had come to see them and break the news that she would be marrying a Frenchman, her elderly father had opposed it, ranting and raving and making threats, swearing that he'd disown her if she married "that damn Christian." He even started talking at length about halal and haram, about God and hellfire. Meanwhile her mother was wailing and cursing the day she'd given birth to a female child, in mourning for the days when girls were buried alive at birth.

But then, in a typically Moroccan mercurial shift, all of that was forgotten, swept away by the changes rushing in. The decrepit furniture in their home had always been shared with rats and cockroaches, as well as being the established and secure breeding ground for generations of spiders; the only thing the house had lacked to complete the picture was Dracula himself. But then it was all replaced. Their father started wearing a full suit and tie instead of his tattered djellaba and smiling foolishly, proud of the daughter who had brought him his millions. A bottle of wine, some weed, and he became so utterly different that he may as well have sprouted a pair of devil's horns out of his head. Flat out on his back, gibbering woozily in delight, he'd say over and over, "A man who has a daughter has a grima." And the phrase "God be pleased with you, Daughter" was constantly on his lips. Even his mother took to rolling up her sleeves in front of her female neighbors to show off her gold bracelets and rings, reveling in the sight of the women's eyes popping out of their heads at that mesmerizing yellow glow. She'd look over at her daughter and say, "The wedding's soon!"

So how long would he go on opposing his sister's

marriage? She would marry the Christian whether the family liked it or not. And he wasn't exactly some modern-day 'Antar. He wasn't about to kill his sister and spend the rest of his life in prison for the sake of—of what? Morals? Honor? Tradition? He didn't know the color, shape, or taste of any of those things; he'd only heard about them in the stories his grandmother used to tell him to lull him to sleep. So he would just have to apply the logic of the times to his sister's case. He would cast off his face like a discarded garment and don an expressionless metal mask in its place that revealed no shame, just like all those other people around him did every day.

He began reciting randomly selected ayahs and hadiths to everyone as a way of making his sister's wedding halal. The neighbors did gossip, of course, but in the end they swallowed their tongues. And why should he justify his behavior to anyone, anyway? People should mind their own business— as the saying went, "God gave each of us our own separate head so that we could leave each other in peace."

He constantly and confidently repeated, within earshot of the other young men in the neighborhood, "It'll just be a few more days, and after that you won't be seeing my face around here again." His dreams were full of his future invasions of all those blond women's beds, for he knew that Moroccan men were like the rest of the Arabs: dirt-poor or loaded, nothing mattered to them except their dazzling victories in bed, and they wouldn't lower their spears or surrender their weapons until they were sure they had dealt the fatal blow and taken down their primary adversary in their life's mission—women. Someday he'd be using broken Arabic, clumsily interspersed with dissonant French words, to tell the others about his affairs with all those creamy-skinned women.

He picked up his crate of cigarettes. He saw the postman and asked him if there was a letter for him from France. The postman answered no without so much as turning toward him. He went into the house cursing everything at the top of his lungs, from his two elderly parents to his sister, who . . .

JUST DIFFERENT

Avenue Mohammed V is silent and desolate this late at night, empty apart from a few stray cats mewling like newborn babies; it's a creepy sound. A she-dog ambles up, stops in front of me, and raises her tail at a black male dog limping past. One bark of seduction from her and he's mounting her. They're cleaved to each other, clinging on, and she shuts her eyes in ecstasy, surrenders to his movements. A delicious tingle runs through me. How lucky they are! They do it in public. They're shameless—as the saying goes, "Not only God sees them but His servants do too." They don't have to worry about a police patrol, or about what people will say.

Bouchta yells, "Kick the shit out of them!"

I take no notice of him. He chucks a stone at the dogs, and when it hits them they both let out a shrill yelp that sounds like a human sob, and then they separate. If I were them I'd attack him, bite his butt cheek.

I've been pacing back and forth along the street for two hours now, and there hasn't been a single customer. It's a drought!

I touch the razor blade in my pocket, checking it's still there. I always keep it on me in case someone suddenly does something sketchy—in case I get cornered. Bouchta stands near Marché Central, leaning against a wall and singing his favorite song in a tuneless croak: "*Red wine, red wine, ah, red wine! The sweetest way to get drunk!*" His coarse voice rips through the still night. He's waiting for his cut. We sweat and stress and bear the repulsive customers, and he doesn't even have to lift a finger. Fuck him and his—

Naimah found a client earlier on, went off on the back of his moped. He seemed like he was probably a worker from one of the factories. "I'm a fan of the working class," she said. "Much better than those beginner drivers you're obliged to teach the ABCs of love. I'm not some practice car for inexperienced pupils to grind around in again and again."

The heel of one of my shoes is hurting me. I can't stand on it for very long at a time. I'd like to go home, drink a little beer, and eat a plate of mussels with hot pepper. That's the best prescription for warming a person up in this cold weather. But Bouchta won't leave me alone. Plus I've got so many expenses: food, clothes, transport, rent. Rent's the main thing. I pay my part for the room I share with Naimah and Skamis. I'm thinking about moving out and living somewhere on my own—I can't stand Skamis anymore. She only needs a couple drinks and she's off, scandalizing us in the street, making a scene. She flips into this crazy, delirious state. She rants, she says all these completely irrational things, she curses everyone and everything out. Things get even worse if she crosses paths with another drunk.

The razor blade's still in my hand: I've been practicing using it ever since I got attacked by those bearded guys who said they wanted to clean up society. Since then I've hated anyone with a beard. "Beardo weirdo," like we say around here. They shaved my head. Bouchta treated me despicably—he just ran away and left me at their mercy. If the police patrol hadn't come by something worse would have happened, for sure. That was the first time I ever felt glad to see a police car: I'd always run from them before, but that day I ran toward them. The loss of my hair still pains me. It was long and blond, like a horse's mane. My mother always loved to brush it, and she'd deliberately let it grow long, right down past my shoulders.

One time my father came back from one of his long trips. He'd go away for months on end, then come home with a few presents for us—perhaps some cheese, a bit of tea—but always plenty of problems. This time he turned up and caught my mom putting lipstick on my cheeks as rouge, my hair pinned up in a bun. He beat her that day till she soiled herself and told her, "You're going to ruin this boy—he'll turn into a fucking sissy."

His hand felt like a pair of metal pliers gripping

my arm as he propelled me along the street to the barber. My hair got shaved down to almost nothing, and I hid my exposed scalp under a blue woolen hat. Back at the house he took the Quran in his hands and recited the Fatiha. He opened his mouth so wide his decayed molars showed, even his tonsils. My heart was pounding, banging against my ribs.

"In the name of God, the most merciful and most compassionate . . ." I began, stumbling over the words.

"Don't you even know the Fatiha, you son of a Zoroastrian?" he sneered, baring his false front teeth.

"You'll go to hell, you dirty little bastard, and it'll be full of women and fags like you."

He gripped the Quran in both hands and smashed it down onto my head. The room spun, the planet Earth spun, and all the heavenly bodies spun too.

"You and your mother will both go to hell! Write out 'I'm a man' a thousand times."

I bent my head and looked down at my hands.

I touched my pinkie: *I'm a man.* I touched my ring finger: *I'm a woman. Man, woman, m— woman.*

I took a piece of paper and sat at the table. He sat near me. His lips never stopped moving; perhaps he was cursing me under his breath, or maybe furiously reciting suras from the Quran? He watched me in disgust, like someone looking at a rotten mouse.

His white cotton gandoura was so soaked in sweat it stuck to his body. I could see his black-and-white striped underwear through it: it looked like zebra skin. I didn't continue looking for very long, to protect myself from his sharp tongue.

"Hands behind him, carrying the devil on his back"—that was what he used to say to me if he caught me with my hands behind my back. But my mother told me when she was brushing my hair one day that men are devils and women are vessels. The Prophet said that women are vessels, and the Prophet doesn't lie. But my father lies: he says that women are vessels with devils hiding inside them.

"What do you want to be when you grow up?"

"A pilot," I said shyly, almost inaudibly.

"A peanut?"

"A piiilooot—with an *l*."

"A pilot, a pilot . . . peee-Lot." He pursed his bluish lips, then stuck them out, sucking his teeth. He frowned, clearly thinking about something weighty, and kept repeating, "*Lot* . . . pee-*Lot*." Then he turned to me and said, "So you want to be in charge of a plane, huh? You won't be in charge of shit, you little hell spawn."

In our Arabic grammar class, the teacher said, "The subject is a 'raised' accusative noun, with an enclosure marked at the end. The object is an 'erect' nominative noun, with an opening at the end."

So I fumbled around at the end of myself, but there was no opening there and nothing raised either. There was something down there about the size of my pinkie, like a little gerbil's tail dangling between my thighs.

The teacher flayed my back with his wooden rod. I groaned. He took off his glasses and cleaned them with the edge of his white teacher's gown. He swept his gaze up and down me, then just down and down me. He had caught me groping that thing of mine that was like a little gerbil's tail. He grabbed me by the shirt collar and threw me out of the classroom, repeating, "There are many children of sin. I won't accept you in my class, unless accompanied by your father." I didn't tell my father anything about it, and I never attended grammar class again after that.

In our Islamic Education class the teacher began, as usual, with, "In the name of God, the most compassionate and the most merciful," followed by, "There is no power and no might except for in God." Invocations done, he then said, "The doer and the one it's done to both burn in hellfire."

His eyes roamed the room and then settled on my face. The other students all looked at me, and I hung my head in embarrassment, as if apologizing for being among them. Their eyes hemmed me in. I was alone among them. Nothing like them. Swathed in sorrow, sweating and shaking. If only I could evaporate, simply disappear.

My friend, unable to contain his sarcasm, quipped, "Madonna, Elton John, and Bouchaib el

Bidaoui will all be in hell to keep you company. Hell's going to be a blast. In heaven, the Islamic Education teacher'll be there and your dad and the religion students from the madrasa. Heaven'll be miserable." He burst out laughing, and just like scabies, it spread to everyone else.

As we were all filing out of the classroom, the teacher made me stay behind. He stroked my face delicately, tenderly, and I doubted his good intentions.

"Your face is smoother than it should be. All your friends have grown mustaches except you." His fingers trembled, sending a shudder through my body. Feelings that were delicious, strange—and sinful. He wiped the droplets of sweat from my brow, his eyes blazing with something strange, like hunger; I lowered my head and left the classroom. His voice followed me out: "You must get on the straight and narrow, the straight and narrow!" His voice sounded like rumbling guts.

The last time I went to wash in the public hammam was years ago. I went during the women's session, put my silver bracelets in the inner pocket of my handbag, and as soon as I started taking off my voluminous black djellaba, the women gathered around me. They pulled my hair. One of them had a knife in her hand and tried to do something embarrassing, rude, and violent with it. And one of them slid her hand down beneath my belly to check something. I was jammed in between their flabby bodies, getting squashed by their breasts and nauseated by the smell of sweat and henna and hair conditioner. By some miracle I got away from them. One of them called after me, "Go to the men's hammam!"

Even out in the street their ululations, their prayers to the Prophet, and their lewd laughter all still reached me. Their anger was a put-on, and so was their yelling.

The next time, I went to the men's session. They grabbed me by the scruff of the neck and threw me out. "Go to the women's hammam!" Whenever I recall that day—the most brutal day of my life—I feel bile rise inside me and I want to puke.

I don't know why they treat me this way: roughly,

rudely, or sometimes with an indifference so extreme it borders on cruelty. In the street they look at me like I'm from another planet, even though the head on my shoulders can't be so different from the rest of the heads around here. Their eyes grow wide; they look confused, then repulsed. They try to suppress their laughter and they let fly that horrible word, but just in a whisper, or in elegant French so as not to ruin the illusion of good taste. There are some who don't know how to address me; they mix up male and female pronouns so their sentences come out sounding ugly, all muddled up and wrong. But what's wrong with the way I look? No one chooses their looks. Haven't they heard the expression "She is one of God's creations"?

The doctor I went to see couldn't stop scratching the tip of his nose and sneezing. After several appointments, a lot of chat and money, and a few tests, he informed me of various things that I couldn't really comprehend: hormones, genes, chromosomes. In the end he told me that I simply needed to accept my body as it was. What a genius!

As if his proclamation would magically solve all my problems. Naimah said the same thing to me in her own way. "Stuff your ears with cotton and live your life the way you want." But how am I supposed to convince the rest of them?

It's 2:00 a.m. now. My fingers are almost completely numb from the cold. Nights like these we call "falso"—just a waste of time. So I'll go home, drink a little beer, and eat a plate of mussels with hot pepper.

THIRTY-SIX*

I hate Saturdays.

I know some people hate every day of the week, and they don't complain. But it's different for me, or at least I think it is.

Every Saturday morning my father shows up very early, dragging his big feet. His swollen paunch clashes with his scrawny build. His face is long and narrow; his forehead bulges with protruding veins. He's not remotely handsome. Each Saturday he has some woman with him I've never met before: she never seems to resemble the woman from the week before, and she'll definitely be nothing like the woman next week either. Today he sends me down

*"Thirty-six" is the numerical code for the Casablanca regional hospital wing for those suffering from mental illnesses.

to Ba Ibrahim's store. It's dark in there, and the stink of decay wafting out makes me nauseous. I don't usually buy our groceries from him. His eyes are crusted and red. He takes a snort of snuff, triggering an endless sneezing fit, then wipes his nose on a grayish handkerchief that looks more like a strip torn off a flour sack, sticky with caked, doughy old snot. He opens the handkerchief, contemplating the contents for a moment, then stuffs it back into his pocket. He tries to muster a few words of welcome, but smiling doesn't suit him. His long, wonky teeth are algae colored. I keep my distance from him and utter a single phrase: "Tall Aïcha." Clamping my arms around my chest, I wait. Our neighbor comes in, her newborn son in her arms. The baby screams insistently and sucks on a bottle of caraway and "woolly cumin" brew. The woman says to Ba Ibrahim, "Take him, the little shit won't shut up." He silences her with an angry gesture of his hand. "He's nothing but an angel," he says. "I have just the right medicine for him." I turn my eyes toward the baby to get a closer look at a real angel. His face is lashless, browless, as if he's suffering from alopecia. He opens his mouth as wide as it will go, screaming violently, his whole face a huge, open mouth, his uvula trembling in his throat like a tiny bell. Ba Ibrahim blows sebsi smoke in the baby's face once, twice, and then he finally falls quiet. The baby's eyes roll back in his head, and he falls asleep. The woman reaches inside her top, releasing a sour odor, brings out a few dirham notes, and holds them out to the shopkeeper, who touches them to his forehead before accepting them. The woman's foul smell must be on the dirhams. The woman thanks him in the kind, gentle way a vinegar-scented woman in her forties would. She leaves, and I repeat my order: "Tall Aïcha." He heads for the back of the shop. I always used to expect him to hand me a gigantic woman when I placed that order, but instead he'd give me two bottles wrapped in newspaper. In that girly voice of his, completely incongruous with his scary appearance, he says, "Straight home now." Then goes back to his usual corner.

Once I was tempted by that blood-red liquid.

I downed the dregs of my father's abandoned glass all in one go. Then I vomited up everything inside me and a revolting smell like rotting socks clung to me for the rest of the day.

My father closes my bedroom door. He's given me half a round flatbread with some canned fish in it. As soon as he's gone I throw it out the window. *I won't lock the door, but don't try to come out.* From the other room wafts the scent of grilling meat; my mouth starts watering. I push the door ajar. Lascivious laughter, rude words, that delicious scent creeping into my nose. My guts go into a frenzy, and it's getting hard to keep my rumbling stomach quiet. I swallow my spit with difficulty, fingering the few dirhams in my pajama pocket. Tomorrow I'll buy half a kofta-and-onion sandwich. Laarbi always looks gross, his big, wobbly belly hanging over his food cart, his fingers up his nose. After he's done digging around for boogers he goes right back to flipping the pieces of kofta and sausage. But it doesn't matter, his food is delicious, and maybe the filth adds to the flavor. He has even more customers crowding around his stall than flies landing on his chopped onion and tomato.

"Dad, I wanna watch television. I wanna see Sinbad. I can't sleep." My grandmother tells my father that cartoons show real-life creatures that live somewhere or other, just like we do. She picks up her prayer beads and goes back to running them through her fingers and softly repeating prayers. The fingers of her other hand don't leave her nostril and don't cease their hopeless attempts to pluck some tiny hairs. Sinbad travels the world on his ship. The djinn comes out of the depths of the sea. The ship capsizes and I fall out of bed. The bedroom is dark. The coat hanger turns into a djinn with outstretched arms coming toward me. I hide my head under the covers. I listen to my heart beating like it's right inside my ear. Where is my mother? I don't see any pictures of her on the walls. There's just a picture of a big monkey wrapping toilet paper around his huge, hairy body, his jaw hanging open idiotically to reveal rusty teeth the size of fava beans. Why does my father insist on hanging that picture in the middle of the hallway? Who was it that said human beings are descended from apes? What does my mother look like? Do I have some of her features? Is she fat? Is she white? I used to carry a notebook around and try to imagine her. I would always draw a woman with no face. One day, on a visit to my grandmother's place in the desert, she said to me, "Your eyes are like your mother's." I was happy: finally, I knew what my mother's eyes were like. Then, picking a louse out of my hair, she added, "Yes—your eyes are completely shameless. As the saying goes, 'Throw a handful of salt in her eyes and she won't even blink.'" My heart was pounding as I wriggled out from between my grandmother's knees. I hated her, and I loved my mother now more than ever.

This Saturday night I feel a searing pain rip through my belly. Something warm is pouring out from between my thighs and running down my legs. It smells foul. I understand, but I don't know what to do. I put my hand between my legs to stop this disgusting contamination from flowing. My fingers are covered in blood. A droplet falls, dark as liver. I shudder, the iron bed frame creaks. My teeth chatter. I feel degraded, humiliated, I'm cringing in abject shame. What if the blood floods the whole room? The stairs? The neighborhood? I cry out. My father comes. His eyes are half-closed. "What's the matter?" His voice sounds like a death rattle. "What's the matter?" His eyes are half-open. "What's the matter?" His face is long and his forehead bulges more than ever. Little curly hairs he wishes would conceal his bald patch. "What's the matter?" His voice gets sharper. Tears like grains of sand, like needles piercing my eyes. "What's the matter?" I want my mom. He pulls off the bedcover, he can see my private parts. My sheets are sopping with blood. My hand is between my thighs. I'm still trying to stop this disgraceful bleeding. It continues. He looks down and his eyes are shards of glass, taking in the scandal-soiled sheets. He looks at my breasts, at the red zits that cover my face. His Adam's apple goes up and down while he scratches the back of his neck; I shake my head from left to right as if defending myself from an accusation. He opens the closet and pulls out an old foot towel. He holds it out for a moment, then chucks it at me, hard. He spits on the floor and leaves the room. I'm still cowering in a ball on the bed. I look at the bloodstain, at the scratchy towel. Here comes the woman who does all that shameless stuff with my father: now she's coming right into my room! She's concealing her nakedness with a white cloth wrap. She laughs a gelatinous, brazen, and mirthless laugh. Then in her smoker's rasp she says, "Come on, best get on with it, you're a woman now." That day I hated my father, I hated my body, and I loved my mother.

The next morning I am woken by the sound of that woman my father brought to the house: she's shouting. I open my puffy eyes and then the door, just a crack. The woman is throwing green banknotes in my father's face, frothing at the mouth, the arteries in her neck bulging. She looks like a frog. "Is that how cheap you think this is?" she yells, gesticulating crudely at the area below her paunch. My father's baggy pants are so low-slung they show half his backside as he rams the notes back into his pocket. He raises his leg to kick her in the butt. "Get out, whore! Women keep the fires of hell burning bright!" The woman dodges the kick and flees. He slams the door behind her with blatant violence.

She keeps on shouting even once she's out in the street: "Haram on you, taking advantage of a hardworking woman—God curse the money you save by cheating me of my dignity, that's a sin!" His eyes are as narrow and tight as two dark little pinpricks, out of proportion with his huge, densely pockmarked nose. He leans his forehead against the wall. I can sense his rage from the rhythm of his breathing. He punches the wall, spits on the floor; I hear him cursing womankind and everything they stand for. The woman is still yelling: she wants her djellaba and her handbag back. He opens her handbag and throws it out the window. Its contents scatter across the asphalt. The children race to steal whatever they can get their hands on as he rips up the djellaba and throws that out the window too. He sits down on the edge of a chair, panting, then laughs in relief.

I can guess what will happen next: he'll go into the bathroom, wash, then he'll turn toward Mecca and say, "I prostrate myself with holy intention, offering an extra prayer to Allah." Every Saturday it's basically the same story on loop. Only a few minor details change from week to week.

Whenever Saturday is getting near, an enormous, heavy stone bears down onto my chest and doesn't budge. I have come to hate Saturdays and to understand why the neighbors call my father "Thirty-six."

WOMAN: A DJELLABA AND
A PACKET OF MILK

My father yells, "Shut your mouth!" at my little boy.
My little boy grows even more alarmed and screams
even louder. I'm in the middle of scrubbing the floor
with an old, rotten burlap rag; I toss it aside and
dry my hands on the side of my brown gandoura.
I cradle my baby, soothing him, crooning, "There
there, my little sweetie." My father spits, and the
spray skims my face. I wipe it off with my sleeve.
"That's it, go on, call him girly names so he turns
out as a pathetic little sissy boy. Demon child. If he
cries anymore I'm throwing him out the window." I
tie my baby onto my back with a large piece of cloth,
give him his pacifier; he spits it out. I know he's
hungry, but there's no milk left. I used to give him
powdered baby formula from the pharmacy, but it
would always run out so fast. I discovered that my

brother was regularly stealing it on his way out to university. When I caught him at it he told me that he would ask the waiter for a cup of water to dissolve the stolen formula into. Then he smacked his lips at the thought of that delicious taste, laughed, and said, "Did *I* drink that kind of milk when *I* was a kid?" After that my father told me, "Just give the baby Centrale milk from the grocery store."

I squeeze my breasts, I wring them out: not a drop of milk. The pharmacist won't give me even one single packet of formula on credit. I said to him, "I'll pay you when the carrot-haired judge with the freckled face rules in my favor." The pharmacist laughed until his bloated body shook; I don't understand why. And now every time he sees me he laughs idiotically and asks me whether the judge has ruled in my favor yet.

I wander through the streets of Casablanca, this slut of a city who opens her thighs to all comers.

Wide streets, cars, chic boutiques displaying very short dresses. The women here are different; you sense they could have just stepped out of a fashion magazine, their bodies luscious, the color of liquid honey. I look at my gray djellaba: I feel insignificant, and I wish I could disappear. I hear my stomach rumbling and remember that I didn't have breakfast this morning. My little boy is on my back, sucking on his bottle filled with tea. The judge's hair is orange, his face is freckled, his beard is patchy, and he never stops fiddling with it. I told him, "I don't want a divorce. I want a house, and a djellaba, and formula milk for my child. My breast milk has dried up, and my father doesn't want the child in his house."

He replied, "Dump the child on his father and go back home on your own." But he's my son! Would anyone actually dump a piece of their own heart? I told my father that I would look for work; he spat in my face—he never stops spitting—then said, "You're not to work, and you're not to stand on the balcony, and you're not to go out on your own. You'll only go to the hammam once a fortnight . . . You're going to become a divorcée."

My child has shrunk to the size of a fragile little doll I'm afraid of breaking. He doesn't stop crying, he wants milk, the pharmacist doesn't want to give me a packet of milk on credit, and the judge with the freckled face doesn't stop fiddling with his beard. My brother steals my son's formula, and my father shouts in my face and spittle flies out of his mouth. And all I want is a room and a djellaba and milk for my baby. Dark thoughts are ruining my life, I'm trying to flee from them, my husband threw me out of the house, and my father gets annoyed by my child's crying. And my mother is enjoying her solitude in that green cemetery. At least she found a place where she could rest. Whenever my problems would overwhelm me I used to take a thermos with some tea in it and two cups and go to that cemetery and sit by my mother's grave, drinking hot tea and eating a piece of bread with homemade butter. The second cup remained forever empty.

Yesterday I stole a blue banknote from my father's wallet and gathered up my clothes—a set of underwear, a headscarf and gandoura—diapers for my baby, and his bottle. I packed everything into a basket and snuck out at night. I caught the first bus to Casablanca. I don't know what devil planted this idea of leaving in my mind! I'm looking out the bus window and watching everything outside falling back away from me: people, trees, buildings. I close my eyes, I don't want to go back.

On the bus everything is for sale: cookies past their expiration date, medicine for eczema and tooth decay and stomach pain, stolen gold rings. Someone is offering cheap rooms, too, in case anyone wants to while away a little not-so-innocent time.

I'm standing in front of a giant building. How many floors does it have? One, two, three . . . ten. I'm getting dizzy, I'm losing count. How many floors? Twenty? Thirty? All I want is a room as big as my body, a djellaba, and some formula for my little boy. What would happen if I went up onto the roof of this building? My baby on my back, my eyes closed, over we go, and I splat onto the asphalt. I wish I knew how a person feels when they're about to die. The dread would distort my face. But what an amazing sensation it would be once I'm flying—flying down. I can guess what would happen after that. People would invent outlandish stories about the reason for my suicide and inflate them until they burst into a proper scandal. My father would curse me both privately and publicly. And my husband-slash-ex—I don't know what to call him, since I'm stuck in limbo—would mournfully usher the well-wishers into his home to offer their condolences. And when they left, he would laugh until he fell over or peed his pants.

But wait! Before all that, while I'm still standing on the roof of this giant building, I'll shout, "I want my husband! I don't love him, and I don't care whether he's around or not, or about his constant infidelity, I just want a roof and four walls and milk for my child." Even when he brought one of his mistresses home that time, I didn't protest. His fist is always quicker than his mouth, like there's a direct line from his ears to his muscles. He is a sadistic character. So I just kept on peeling onions, mopping my eyes and my round nose every so often, until eventually it hurt from so much wiping. When he came into the kitchen, zipping up his pants, he asked me if I was crying out of jealousy. Without raising my eyes, I told him, "No, I was just peeling onions."

He seemed angry and left the house with his mistress. She was dressed in a black djellaba, and she used the pocket slits to deliberately pull the fabric tight around her, showing off her ass. The look in her eyes was brazen and fearless.

The sun seems to be feeling shy, like it always does in March. I'm worn out from walking. I sit down on a rickety bench in a park. My baby clings to my back like a little worm. I laugh at that comparison.

I sneak a look at two men kissing each other on the bench facing mine. I feel my heart pounding. I'm embarrassed. I lower my head. But why should *I* be embarrassed? I look at them again and the sight revolts me; one of them has a smooth face, almost girlish, the other is huge. I touch my own face. It feels rough and dry. They've noticed me. Muttering something, the big one takes his date by the hand, glares, and spits at me before quitting the scene.

Clouds cover the sun. The sun is like a child playing hide-and-seek, hiding and reappearing from time to time. I don't like this grayness: not sunny, not cold, not raining. I hate the color gray. It's a crook of a color, hard to pin down, neither one thing nor the other. My husband was kind of gray: he was always angry, but I never really knew if he loved me or hated me, if he wanted me or wanted me to leave. So I left his house and my father's house and the coastal city that reeks of fish and factory waste.

Damn! How come I gave in to my urge to leave? Should I go back? Yes, I'll go back, I'll kiss my father's hand and say to him . . . No, I won't say anything to him, he can go to hell, he couldn't stand my little boy, he never even called him by his name. He used to always call him "son of a Doukkali," then get stuck into meting out foul insults about the people of Doukkala, his favorite topic.

I can't bear this hunger anymore. I open my basket and take out a piece of harcha I brought with me. The bread is cold, but never mind. I remember my mother, who made the best harcha. The women of the neighborhood would gather around a steaming pot of mint tea at aseria time, she would set out the harcha she'd made, and the gossip would commence. Those wonderful afternoon gatherings used to fly by, and then they were gone for good.

A piece of meat is sitting opposite me, pretending to read a newspaper; he keeps looking over at me. A drop of water falls on my nose. Two drops fall. He takes off his glasses, puts them back on, smiles, winks. He looks like a clown trying to be kind. I pick a wilted rose and fiddle with its petals: *I'll go back home . . . I won't go back . . . I'll go back,* and finally the sky stops dithering and lets out a downpour. Damn it! Damn it! I hug my child to my chest, the man calls out to me and waves his keys, the wilted rose whimpers between my fingers: *I'll go with him, I won't . . . I'll go with him . . .*

A WOMAN IN LOVE,
A WOMAN DEFEATED

I went to the seer, held the playing cards to my chest, and chanted the invocation after her: "Here's my heart, reaching for guidance . . ."

She belched a lot. She told me that a spell had been put on me and him to make him run off. But she guaranteed me he'd be back, and said I'd then be obligated to pay for a "big slaughter" and a "Gnawa night." I didn't really understand what a "big slaughter" meant, but I nodded my head anyway. Then she arched her eyebrows, closed her eyes, and started moving her lips very rapidly, talking to people only she could see. She informed me a black djinn named Mimoun had taken up residence in my body and was the cause of everything that had happened to me. The very idea that I could be sharing this skinny body with a mischievous black djinn horrified me. I left her chicken coop–sized house. The smell of incense had gotten into my clothes. Damn it!

In return for the bundle of banknotes the seer took from me, I received a candle. Her house was in a maze of winding, branching alleyways. And now I was about to enter another maze and other wars with djinns and afarit—as if my battles with humans weren't enough to be dealing with already that I needed to get embroiled in battles with a djinn! I did light the candle as instructed, so as to reignite his love, but he didn't show up. I started thinking seriously about putting on a Gnawa night and making a pilgrimage to the shrine of the marabout Bouya Omar.

I look out my bedroom window. My cat has trouble walking now because her stomach is even more swollen than before. It's the size of a pear. Ever since my father threw her out of the house, I've fed her in secret. She left home a while back, chasing after a scabby tom who had seduced her, and then later she came back, rubbing herself up against me again like nothing had happened. I did the same thing, left everyone behind and followed him. He wasn't handsome. He looked like a little bald bear with a saggy paunch hanging down past his genitals, and he had a huge ass and a round face. I always hated men with huge asses and round faces. So how did I fall in love with him? Love is like that, it always shows up without an appointment. Love is like death, like illness, always arriving when we least expect it, at the most peculiar times and places. Love makes us behave like irrational children. Why can't they just invent a vaccine against it?

I feel cold. I look up at the dark sky: it's been abandoned by the stars. It's going to rain for sure. I sneeze three times; I'm coming down with a cold. I don't like winter, rainy season of red noses and muddy streets. When I was little I used to love it. I'd go out with the neighborhood kids and we'd bellow, with a joy unmatched by any other, "Ashtatata, pour, pour, pour, pour your rain down." Now Naima Samih's voice coming from the little radio is warped and slack; the batteries are almost dead: "*Oh my wound! This wounded wandering, this endless enduring.*"

He doesn't like Naima Samih, or Umm Kulthum. He says songs like that make him yawn. I calibrated my life to his desires and his whims and his moods. We never went out except when he wanted to. We never went anywhere unless it was somewhere he felt comfortable. My desires, my moods . . . never mind. It doesn't matter anymore. From now on . . .

I listen to the dawn call to prayer. I get goosebumps all over my body; the hairs on my arms are standing on end. The dawn azan makes me feel like weeping. I wish I could cry loudly and kick my feet against the ground like I used to when I was a little girl, so that my mom would come and put me on her lap and rock me and sing softly to me, "*Allah, Allah . . . Mohammed is Allah's messenger,*" until I calmed down and fell asleep. I hear my mother's footsteps as she heads toward the bathroom to make her ablutions before prayer. My father only prays during Ramadan. When I asked him why he doesn't pray the rest of the year, he told me he believes in God, and that's enough—he doesn't need to prove it five times a day.

When he came to ask for my hand and my mom had a look at him through the slit of the door, she clapped her hands to her cheeks so hard the impact printed ten red fingers on her face, and she said, "Uff, he's no looker, and he's taken his sweet time!" *But Mom, aren't you always saying, "A covered head is better than a bare head," plus—I'm in love with him!* She peeped at him again. He was handsome in his yellow shirt. I remembered that I hate the color yellow, the color of rotten yellow teeth and hypocritical yellow smiles, and Lalla Mira, the djinn queen who loves yellow. My father seemed displeased as well. He started fiddling with the lone clump of four hairs sprouting from his chest. He blew cigarette smoke in my face and said, "This is a shoddy deal!"

But Dad, since when are emotions added up on a calculator? Am I talking to my father or a trader in the scrap market?

He looked at me, then added, "And he's a state

clerk." He enunciated the phrase like a curse or an accusation. *But I'm in love with him.* He shrugged and said, "Go to hell. Shameless generation!"

What about you, Dad, aren't you embarrassed that you married me off when I was still just a kid with pigtails? You made a fat profit that day, didn't you, getting me married—or should I say selling me off. I remember how my mother took me to the hammam. She washed my body, plucked my armpit hair and my pubic hair, and told me things that turned my face red with shame. And the women dyed my hands with henna and put kohl around my eyes. Their ululations sounded like screams and wailing laments. And after that I found myself facing a very tall man. The first thing he did was slap me and say, "The cat dies on day one," and I knew that, in this context, I was the cat. That's all I know about marriage: hammam, henna, ululations, and a man who slaps you to prove he's stronger than you. And after that he fills your belly with kids and hits the road.

My first husband fled and left me in the shit.

And then this one, the one I was in love with, he ran off as well—once again I was back in the shit. They all vanish as soon as things get serious.

My mother grimaces, her lower lip curling, and asks why he disappeared. The black djinn is still living inside my body; my sister sticks her tongue out and thumbs her nose at me. The seer says, "You need a Gnawa night and a big slaughter and lots of cash." She puts the banknotes between her breasts, lights a Casa brand cigarette, and demands submission. My neighbor says the seer used to be a cheikha, and then when times got hard she became a soothsayer.

I'm hungry. I put on my slippers. I'll go to the kitchen and eat a pancake smeared with honey. I turn back at the last moment. I must quit this bad habit. When I'm angry the only place I can vent my anger is the kitchen. Sometimes I cry as I gorge myself on anything and everything. I must look pathetic, and disgusting. Afterward I go to the bathroom and stick my fingers down my throat and get rid of it all.

I have to be strong. This time I won't vent my fury by eating. I'll go to see him at his workplace and stick my tongue out at him and say, "The universe doesn't begin and end at your feet."

I'll say to him, "I regret giving you more love and respect than you deserve."

I'll tell him, "I regret being ready for anything with you, while you weren't ready for anything except lying and hypocrisy, so here's to you! Congratulations on being the best liar around."

Tomorrow I'll burn his photos and letters, his gifts and his lies. And I won't light the candle again to reignite his love and bring him back to me. I won't put on a Gnawa night.

Ufff, I'm hungry—I'll eat just one pancake, no more than that. I wonder how much a Gnawa night actually costs anyway?

RAVING

He kissed my cracked lips.

"A paternal kiss . . . you are like a daughter to me."

I run my tongue over my lips. Oozing, something sticky. Blood . . . saliva? Who knows.

Someone is shining a bright light into my eyes . . . I'm trying to open them . . . I can't.

My head is weighed down . . . I try again . . . I close them again . . . Where exactly am I?

The man told me after he gnawed at my lips, "A paternal kiss . . . you are like a daughter to me."

But my father doesn't kiss me on the mouth . . . in fact, he has never kissed me ever. Or maybe he did when I was a baby? Does my father kiss my mother? I close my eyes, I'm squeezing them tightly shut, I'm picturing him: a gray djellaba . . . yellow slippers with a dusting of earth, a huge turban like a satellite dish . . . my mother stands facing him, I'm trying to picture her . . . slender, wearing a crimson kaftan, locks of white-streaked black hair showing under her little kerchief. When my mother got angry she would shout at us, "You've turned my hair white before its time!"

My big, tall father bends down to put his hands around my mother's waist . . . and the image disappears . . . like the picture on our old television. All my father's fury gathers in his fist, he punches the TV and the picture comes back . . . he laughs victoriously: "Spare the rod, spoil the child."

Where am I? Am I there? And who is that man who chewed on my lips and when I tried to stop him, said, "a paternal kiss."

I run my tongue over my lips; they taste like burned plastic.

When Salah used to kiss me I wanted him to go on and on doing it, into infinity. I loved how his kisses tasted . . . of cigarettes and cheap wine. When he quit smoking and drinking, I had no appetite for his kisses anymore. I would be sniffing him, searching for that smell I had grown addicted to, not finding it . . . Desire slunk off to a safe distance and I slipped out from between his hands. He got angry and yelled in my face, "You've changed! Are you in love with someone else?"

"Have you got a cigarette and some cheap wine?"

Stunned, he turned pale.

"Have you started sm-sm-smoking?"

"No, but you—you should smoke before our dates, every time. And can you gargle with booze, too? I'm addicted to that smell."

He laughed until there were tears in his eyes. "I feel like my chest is a cage full of birds, all squawking at once—you'll land me straight in the oncology ward!"

Where am I? Is it possible that I'm there?

Will someone come to ask me, *Who is your god? What is your religion? Who is your prophet?*

Whoever has the magic answer will spend the rest of their life/death in . . .

A TV show on one of the self-broadcast

channels says, *If you have the answer to our questions . . . call now! This could be your lucky day, win a trip to—*

Where am I? Laid out on my back as if I'm in the morgue . . . one of my hands has needles in it, I can't move, my head hurts, I manage to move my right hand, no wait, it's my left . . . I grope for my body beneath the bedcover, or is it a shroud?

I touch my breast, wincing . . . it's like a fried pepper, limp and revolting. A month after I met Salah, a month or a week . . . maybe it was only hours . . . he said to me, "I want to touch your breasts."

His request shocked me.

"I feel like your breasts aren't real. They're unnaturally round, it's like they're inflated. Are they really your breasts, or is your bra padded? Can I feel them?"

I laughed at this, at the time. I held back for a moment and then said, "Today you want to check my breasts are real, tomorrow my thighs, and then what? It'll never end."

I love his body. It's like a piece of charred wood,

I cling to him even harder, I melt under the heat of his lips, he breaks my ribs with his arms . . . Is it true he has an extra rib?

When I said to my husband, *I want you*, he said, *You are badly brought up . . . aren't you ashamed to talk that way?*

The next day he said to me, *I want you.*

I said to him, *You are badly brought up . . . aren't you ashamed to talk that way?*

He laughed stupidly. *This is my right—as granted to me by my religion and by my forefathers.*

When he forced me to do it, I surrendered woodenly. He shouted in my face, *Am I married to a statue?*

When I moaned in his arms and writhed and whispered sexy things, he shouted in my face, *Who taught you that? Who touched you before me?*

Salah wasn't interested in asking stupid questions, or permitting and forbidding things on a whim.

I shouted and shouted and shouted . . . I left the house, shouting . . . I ran through the alleys, shouting ... I heard the screech of tires ... my body fell violently onto the asphalt, and I wasn't shouting anymore.

Where am I?

My mother comes, puts her hand on my head, and starts murmuring some Quranic suras.

"Where am I?"

"You're in the hospital."

"Mom, he kissed me, his eyes were the color of diseased liver, and when I pushed him away he said, 'You're like a daughter to me.' He was wearing white clothes. Was he a nurse? A doctor? Or a butcher? Are we in a butcher's shop, Mom?"

"Sleep, my girl, you're raving ..."

CLAUSTROPHOBIA

They warned me. They let me know me that catching the number three bus was a risky undertaking
with potentially dangerous consequences. *Suffocated
on the way in and pickpocketed on the way out.* But
I laughed and insisted, like a temperamental idiot,
on giving it a go. I bought my ticket at the ticket
booth and waited for the bus. I could probably
have reached any country in the Arab world in less
time than it took the auspicious bus to turn up.
And no sooner had that ungainly and unattractive
thing lumbered into view than a human flood went
streaming toward it, shouldering and kicking each
other, some taking shortcuts by jumping acrobat-
ically in through the windows. I don't even know
how I got on. All I knew was that my body was
wedged in tightly between scores of other bodies

moving toward the bus: I certainly wasn't walking. So how did I get on? I really don't know.

In front of me was a woman with a child on her back of about four years old, indifferent to what was going on around him, munching on a greasy doughnut and slurping from time to time on the snot running out of his nose. To my left was someone with body odor so nauseating it could knock a person out. And behind me was someone pressing up against me in a weird way. I could feel his breath burning my ear. The decrepit bus moved like a time-ravaged tortoise, the driver pulling over to let scores more humans on at every stop. I don't know how the bus had room for that colossal number of passengers.

The man's breaths were still too close to my ear. I tried to pull away from him a little, but it was so jam-packed in there—such claustrophobia, such a stink of sweat and farts. The man was blatantly rubbing himself up against me, and if I stayed silent any longer it would be taken to mean I was enjoying the game. *You bastards—even on the bus?*

"Hey, brother . . . Oi, you! Can you give me some space? It's rude, what you're doing, shame on you. You really can't think of a better place to do that than here?"

"I'm not doing anything, it's just crowded in here . . . and anyway, someone's squashing me from behind, too, and I'm keeping quiet. I'm putting up with it."

"If you're enjoying this game that's your business, but I'm not."

"If you don't like it, get off the bus and take a taxi."

Growls and snarls and expletives rumbled around the bus. The driver thundered, "Silence! Or I'm rerouting the bus to the nearest police station!"

For God's sake! I desperately wanted to get out of there. What devil gave me the idea of taking this damn bus? The tortoise stopped for the tenth time. No, it wasn't a tortoise anymore: it had become a mythical beast now, devouring this immense quantity of people.

I heard a raised voice. Crammed in this tight between the passengers, there was no way I could see who was at the front or the back of the bus.

"Brothers, sisters, I'm a ruined man: I have ten kids . . . and nothing to feed them . . ."

Another voice yelled, "Ruined and poor, you bastard, and you father ten kids? You should be strung up, not bailed out!"

"The rich fill their time with their sports clubs and foreign travel, while these lowlife scum fill the void between their wives' thighs and play checkers."

"I know him, he lives in Derb Ghallef. He's not married! He's always showing up with some new story to get people feeling sorry for him."

The smell of sweat and farts, that kid in front of me savoring his snot feast with such an appetite that I felt sick to my stomach, the increasingly scary panting of the beast behind me, and before I knew what I was doing, I shouted, "I want to get out!" And finally I did it. I don't know where exactly, but whatever. I filled my lungs with air. Polluted air, sure, but a hundred times better than the air inside that bus.

I flagged down a taxi. I thanked God when I arrived home. When I went to pay the fare, I discovered my wallet was gone. It had disappeared from my bag.

BLOOD FEAST

First of Ramadan, April 14, 1990

To Karima:

Shakespeare said, "Let us not burden our remembrances with a heaviness that's gone."

But someone like me must remain burdened with her remembrances, so as not to forget how, that Ramadan, you cut out a piece of your body to grant me life. How would I ever flee from you, when you dwell in me?

I took the glass tube the doctor gave me and ducked into the restroom of the government hospital. Rank, putrid stench. My swollen fingers held my nose, fending off that overwhelming odor. Unlike my wife, I'm not generally a fan of sitting around in restrooms—it's her favorite place to leaf through a cookbook. I handed the sample back to the doctor. As she contemplated the murky, blood-streaked liquid, she made a face, whether in anguish or in disgust I couldn't say.

About a month ago—no, not a month, actually; it's been exactly twenty days, it was just a week after my wedding—I started having pain in my lower back. Extremely intense pain. Racking me, consuming me, paralyzing me, spreading to my belly, to my bladder. I would crawl to the bathroom, where the task of peeing had now become a grueling operation, brown droplets trickling out and burning like hot chili pepper. My grandmother blended up her own peculiar herbal tonics, bitter and repulsive, and forced great gulps of them down my gullet. The neighbors, too, began inventing recipes and bringing their own outlandish concoctions to the house, so that I became a lab rat with a puffed-up face as yellow as if it had been tinted with turmeric.

My mother said, "The bride walked the bad luck in." But according to the Soussi faqih, a toukal curse had been put on me. He took off my clothes, his blue lips moving, his eyes opening and closing. I felt weak. He fiddled with my body. *Fuck you, if I had my full strength I'd break your bones!*

That pain is back again, I'm shouting and screaming, the faqih says it's toukal, my mother accuses my wife . . . my wife shrinks back, fearful, weeping . . . swears on the holy book that she hasn't hurt me . . . she and my sister are swearing at each other, trading insults and cursing my mother, until it turns into a fistfight . . . meanwhile, I'm corpse-like on my back, feeling like I'm suffocating. The doctor touches my body with her cold hands, pressing on my back, my stomach, my bladder, everywhere. All of me. I'm embarrassed, I blush. She doesn't. She's used to this. Her face is rectangular and paper white. If my grandmother saw her she would give her one of her weird concoctions to put some color in her cheeks.

I lay on the hospital bed. It was even more putrid than the restroom. Dried gunk on the bedding, pee stains . . . I groaned. A person lying on the next bed over looked at me, sucking on a cheap cigarette, trying to conceal it from the head nurse. He said to me, "You'll be back." The doctor had said the same thing, "You'll be back." She had informed me that I was suffering from chronic kidney failure. I shrugged, indifferent. Is that any worse than having a dodgy appendix? I didn't think so. Surely it'd just be a question of some pills, and maybe an injection, for a week or a month or whatever, and then I'd be "healthy as a horse," as my mother likes to say about me. I'd be going home to my house in Beni Mellal, where my wife was waiting for me. That'd be that. And we'd make half a dozen kids.

But the doctor said things I wasn't used to hearing, things that sounded strange to my ears: *dialysis, artificial kidney, tubes, a simple operation on the arm,* and *you'll be at the hospital twice a week, you'll come back to Casablanca from Beni Mellal.* My father said, "What've you got, AIDS? If it's kidney trouble I'll take you to Sidi Harazem. No one's ever gone there without getting cured. Anyway, I don't trust that doctor—women aren't cut out to be doctors. And how are your kidneys making you feel like you can't breathe well enough to sleep at night? You're asthmatic, that's what's wrong with you."

The pain is back, more ferocious now, even crueler, stops me from thinking and concentrating. Should I listen to what the doctor says, or go with what my father says? The man lying on the next bed— sucking on that cheap cigarette of his, making me feel even shorter of breath than I did already—said to me, "You don't have the right to choose life; your only choice is between dying immediately, all up front, or dying in installments over the course of months and years. Death will steal in through your pores; it'll eat into your bones and your chest and your heart, and eat from the same plate as you, and creep into you on the air you breathe. And eventually you'll get used to its presence; you'll start to feel more at ease having it around. You'll befriend it. But because death is a cowardly traitor, it'll come at you from behind and betray you: Azrael will play his game with you when you're least expecting him— he always comes when we're least expecting him! And they'll take you to your grave and weigh your body down with a big rock to make sure you don't come back, and shed a couple tears over you, and then eat a delicious couscous and drink a lot of black coffee while wishing mercy on your soul—right as you're submitting the ledger of your behavior in this mortal world for judgment."

He was silent for a while. He stubbed his cigarette out irritably and then immediately lit another, his hands trembling. I wished I could ask him to stop smoking, and talking, and even breathing . . . The pain was tearing into me again and my body hurt as if I'd covered thousands of kilometers on foot. As the pain flared, my friend's words flared along with it: "Life is a whore: she runs from you if you pursue her and show a bit of interest in her, but comes crawling to you on her knees if you've turned your back on her and fled.

"And my wife is a whore. Goddamn them, women, every one of them, from Eve to my wife—all except my mother. Before the illness I was the boss: I called the shots, and my wife didn't dare raise her voice in front of me. I would give her this look, I only needed to look at her once and she would retreat to the kitchen. Can you believe that she used to wash my feet every day? But when the illness got hold of me and my body stopped working, she turned into Nimrod and dominated me. I hardly spoke, and I struggled to get up on my feet and then struggled to sit back down again. At the end of a kidney session I'd be like a wet rag, dragging my skinny body home to crumple in a heap on the bed, so tired I only wanted one thing: sleep. I could no longer work, my health totally fucked me over, and she became the man of the house—she was the one working, that was how come she ruled over me like a tyrant. I'll whisper a secret in your ear, well it's not really a secret anymore . . . she scandalized me, damn her, that bitch! I couldn't satisfy her in bed anymore. I'd get tired so quickly, I'd be tired before I even got started. I'd be sweating all over and my heart would almost stop beating. So I would avoid her. In the beginning she used to berate me with her eyes, just a look, but then it turned into ugly public insults. That destroyed me. One night I tried to overcome my weakness with Viagra. Those pills restored me to my former glory—and even to the glory of my forefathers! The battle was over, but it ended in the ER. It was a humiliating incident that only someone as far gone and useless as me would understand. After that I told her to do whatever she wanted but to keep it out of my sight. I didn't want to know. Not that she had been waiting for permission from me anyway: news of her affairs was already reaching me. My parents nearly lost their minds. But for me to accept a situation like that, I'd need a heart made of mule dung and veins running with pig piss instead of blood.

"So I had to divorce her, to preserve whatever tiny scraps still remained—if anything—of my supposed manhood. But that depraved whore scandalized me in front of the entire family; she told them that I was just like a woman, that she was more of a real man than me . . . the lowbred bitch."

He lit another cigarette from the butt of the one he'd been smoking. He continued, even chattier now:

"But anyway, let's talk about something more important than women—they don't deserve all this attention from us, they're just a crooked rib that breaks if you try to straighten it. The crucial thing is what I'm about to tell you right now: you must get your treatment for free. Even in the government hospital a kidney session is super expensive. There are only a few benefactors who contribute to the costs of treatment. Their secretary will ask you for some documents. Oh, and speaking of the secretary, every time I see her I feel like she's been put together wrong—don't laugh—her face is like an old yellow slipper, and she's cross-eyed, and her mouth is crowded with pointy teeth like a shark; her breasts droop and sag, she's got a massive ass, and her legs are like two thin sticks. Anyway . . . she'll ask you for a certificate proving your poverty, and another proving your illness, and some photos of you. The 'major' won't give you the poverty certificate unless you get with the program and stick your hand in your pocket and pull out something like a fifty-dirham note—even though he knows better than anyone that you are poorer than poverty itself. Then once she's put the file together the secretary will give you a number: you'd better learn it by heart, because from then on you'll be nothing but a number. Your number could be 100, or it might even be 1,000. And you'll wait a year or two, maybe even three. My friend waited three years, and when his turn came to receive free treatment he had already surrendered his soul to its maker. But if you're lucky and you know someone whose name can split rocks, then a miracle will take place on this earth—instead of your number being 1,000, they'll cross out the three zeros so that you're number one, and you'll immediately be granted free treatment. So rack your brains, try to remember if you ever knew somebody, anybody, even just someone who's what we call 'the whiff of fat on the cleaver,' has some remote connection to a member of parliament or a minister, someone to pull some strings for you. Maybe you know a certain dancer?

"You'll learn how to kiss hands and feet, you'll beg and bow and crawl, you'll prostrate yourself, go as low as it takes to plead for the price of treatment. Because if you don't do that, you'll sell everything you own—that is, if you actually own anything in the first place. And you'll get into debt and you'll see how your friends and your parents and your children all run from you; bit by bit you'll sell off your very bones, and your blood drop by drop, to cover the cost of treatment. Don't get me started about the government, making out like they don't know what goes on—they know everything, what we keep private and what we make public—they even know what goes on in bed between someone and their spouse. But they look the other way; they ignore our existence. Once, many years ago, I don't remember exactly when, an official came to the hospital; he smiled for the TV cameras, and pictures were taken of him kissing a sick little girl. The photos were printed on the front pages of some of the national newspapers. And after that he talked a lot of big talk, and we believed him and clapped for him and smiled—we practically wept at his kindness. But whenever we went to him to ask him to keep his promises, he wasn't in, or he was in a meeting . . . or . . . or . . . It took a while, but eventually we understood that our job was done. We'd applauded him and given him our blessing, sung his praises in front of the TV cameras, and we would not be needed further. That experience taught us not to applaud anything and everything. Of course on the rare occasion that one of the officials would remember us again and pass by, escorted by his subordinates and his cameras and his journalists, they would oblige us to attend and smile and clap, in all our disgust. And afterward we would turn away and leave, without waiting for anything or expecting anything. We finally understood the rules of the game."

My friend went silent. Having spewed his poison

onto me, he could finally shut up. Inside my head I was cursing him. Why couldn't he just let me work everything out for myself? He started humming a chaabi song. The secretary came in. I knew her at once—the sagging, droopy bosom, the giant ass. In the husky voice of a smoker, she told me, "You must provide a certificate of poverty, a certificate proving your illness, and . . . well . . . until your turn comes, you'll be liable for all treatment costs yourself." I looked at my friend. He smiled bitterly and nodded his head. I stuffed my swollen feet into my slippers and dragged my weary body out of the hospital.

I was trying to shout, then I really was shouting, "Where am I supposed to get the money to pay you?" I came to: everyone was looking at me. I heard one of them say, "That man's gone crazy." Had I really?

A DAY IN THE LIFE OF A MARRIED MAN

Dull, dull, dull. The same thing happens every day, in the same way and at the same time: I go to work, she goes into the kitchen, I come home at lunchtime, she prepares the meal, we eat in silence, we exchange a few words. *The weather is stifling, the heat is unbearable,* and in winter, *the weather is freezing, the cold is unbearable.*

I try to push her into conversation, any old conversation, just so long as we don't stay silent. I fail, I try again, I fail, I go back to work, she goes back into her kitchen, washes dishes, wipes down the stove, chats on the phone, runs up a bill that electrocutes me. At night she makes dinner, we eat in silence, we exchange the same few words: *the weather is stifling, the heat is unbearable,* or in the best case she might add a sentence or two, grumbling about

my mother, who visited her, or about my sisters, or
... or ...

I bury my head in a newspaper. She watches TV, flicking through the channels in obvious irritation. I ignore her. Rawboned fashion models, my God, don't they eat? The outfits they wear are so weird it's like they're from another planet. I sneak a look at my wife. She's always munching on something or other, chewing away. Thick folds of fat have clumped around her neck and her waist, but her legs are still as skinny as a goose's. I take in the terrain of her body, the highland peaks, the lowland valleys. In this changing landscape, her backside is still as flat a plain as ever. It all feels so repetitive, I'm pining for the days of our betrothal ... Uff ...

I feel this routine choking me, like a poison I'm taking by the spoonful. It's running through my veins, slowly spreading around my body, paralyzing me ... it's suffocating me, and yet death never comes.

She ostentatiously heaves herself to her feet, goes into the bedroom. She calls to me in a voice she's trying to make sound seductive. I know what she wants. I ignore her. She repeats her call, trying and failing to make her voice soft and tender. I pretend to be searching for something, I don't know exactly what. She is still calling for me.

Her tone this time is laced with menace . . . I surrender my fate to Allah and reluctantly drag my body into the bedroom. I find her spread out on her back like a mangy dolphin. Even the way we do *this* is dull . . . no excitement and nothing new, even in bed. The smell of onion and garlic mixed with cinnamon makes me feel like I'm sleeping inside a stew pot, or in a spice store, makes me completely lose any desire I might have felt. I turn my back to her. I can guess the laundry list of Moroccan swear words she must be rattling off inside her head. You try making a woman go hungry sexually! Just try depriving her of her rights in bed—whatever the reason—and suddenly her claws will come out. You'll become an utterly loathsome person in her eyes, someone who provokes her fury on sight, who talks in a vapid way, with a repugnant mustache and an irritating mother and bitter spinster sisters who've made her life hell—she'll turn you into a monstrous freak devoid of one single commendable feature, and she'll curse everyone who conspired to "make the match and make the marriage." A woman might let many things go unpunished, such as your empty bank account or your lack of interest in buying her a birthday present—she'll even take a smack across the face dealt in a moment of anger—but she will definitely not overlook being denied her rights in bed . . . Even if you set her up in the most luxurious villa and dressed her in the trendiest styles and gifted her her body weight in gold, all that would count for nothing. She will seek out whatever ways she can to make your life hell, no matter what. The phrase "You've never once brightened my day" will become her refrain, repeated night and day in every rhythm and to every tune until you're obliged to grant her a divorce. And if she isn't able to get by financially without you and is forced to stay with you for that reason, you can be sure that she'll cheat on you with the person closest to you, perhaps your driver.

Something else I want to whisper in your ear: women are really masochists by nature. Don't let your mouth hang open like that. A woman loves an evening beating from time to time, before she goes to sleep, and for you to pull her hair every once in a while—these customs have been ingrained in women since the Stone Age. And when she complains about it to her neighbor, don't you believe her cries of misery. She's just doing that to spite her neighbor, as an indirect way of telling her, "My husband hits me, therefore he cares about me." The neighbor will purse her lips at this, outraged and indignant, and goad her on to stand up to her husband, informing her that only donkeys are still getting beaten like that in this country, and afterward she'll go home (the neighbor), and you can be sure she'll create some problem or other, do whatever it takes to provoke her husband and drive him out of his mind, and she won't let it go until she gets her evening dose and obtains the indisputable proof she can offer the next day to her neighbor: that she too has a husband who cares about her.

Note: don't try this prescription with all women.
But that's enough off-limits talk for one day.

HEAD LICE

To my counterpart in privation: The Awaited Mahdi, Mohammed al-Mahdi Saqal

If he'd obeyed me I wouldn't be here now, and he wouldn't be there either . . . but he's what we call "head-cracking stubborn."

Lice and stench and cockroaches. I thought head lice died out ages ago, but in this dump they're still going strong. The flabby woman sitting across from me is picking through her friend's hair. From time to time she yells out, "There's one. I've got it!" She squashes each little nit between her two thumbnails.

My mother used to put my head on her lap, too, and search for those tiny little bugs. She'd arm herself with a bottle of paraffin and one of those old-fashioned combs made from sheep or gazelle horn, and then she'd launch her attack on the parasites feeding on my blood. I'd try to wriggle away, she'd grab my arms, I'd keep struggling. Eventually she'd lure me in with *I'll tell you the tale of Hayna, who was abducted by a ghoul*—and at that I'd surrender instantly.

The other woman sitting opposite me—her face is as yellow as sulphur, that's why they nicknamed her Eggy—sticks her hand down between her breasts, pulls out a little packet, and opens it. Lots of cigarette butts. She considers carefully which one to choose, picks it out, and then asks for a match from a brightly colored woman (and I'm not calling her "colored," I'm not racist, she is just wearing very colorful clothes) who passes her one without interrupting the song she's singing: *"No well was ever richer, but how dry is our own pitcher!"*

The young woman tries to slip out of the flabby woman's grasp, who yells, "You're covered in lice, girl, let me zap them for you!"

"Zap your own lice already!"

I'm trying to escape my mother's grip. She

adjusts her hold on me and opens the bottle of paraffin she bought from al-Saidi, the coal merchant.

I close my eyes so that the paraffin doesn't get in them; my mother goes on with the story: *Hayna was beautiful, she had hair as long and thick as a horse's mane, and as soft as silk . . .* Droplets of paraffin are trickling down my neck. The fumes are so pungent. I hold my nose.

Mommy, I don't like paraffin and I don't like lice and I don't like al-Saidi! I'm crying. "Don't cry," says the flabby woman. "They won't put you away for more than six months."

The yellowish woman comes over, offers me a cigarette stub. "Here, you have this, I can spare it."

"I don't smoke," I tell her, my head on my knees.

Last time I messaged him I said, Why don't you try to understand my point of view?

—Because what you say isn't rational.

I'd seized the keyboard and typed, He who can't afford to marry, let him fast from the carnal feast.

—I've tried fasting, but then someone always asks me, "Why are you fasting? Is it some religious occasion?" That immediately makes me think about my body, and I feel even more pressure.

—The fornicator and the adulteress both burn in hellfire.

—Well, God forgives all sins except polytheism, right?

—What will happen when we lock ourselves in your room?

—I'm no soothsayer . . . but I might be a prophet. I'll be your Christ. Didn't Christ raise the dead?

—I'm scared.

This message has not been delivered to all of the intended recipients because they seem to be offline.

I feel frustrated.

The smell of cigarettes is choking me, the paraffin fumes are making my head spin. I feel like puking. My mom quits dousing me with paraffin and carries on with her story: *One day, Hayna was out gathering firewood with her girlfriends when the rain came streaming down from the sky in torrents, and oh, the thunder and lightning! Ya lateef.*

I'm trembling.

It's still raining outside, I tell him. He holds me close, and I lay my head on his bare chest.

You won't feel cold in a minute . . . I'm about to redraw the map of your body with my fingers.

I smile. I flee to the farthest corner of the room, my mom catches up with me and grabs me, wins herself continued access to my hair with the next installment of her tale: *Hayna was happy, for after a long drought the rain had come to irrigate the land and slake the livestock's thirst. But after a little while a black cloud came sweeping over, and she didn't manage to run away like her friends did, poor girl. That black cloud was actually a ghoul who abducted Hayna and ran off with her far faaaarrr away.*

The officer gropes my butt on his way past, pretending it's an accident, says, "Cover yourself, whore." That's how he addresses me while he devours me with his eyes.

I needed to silence the cry of my body, I would have liked to tell him.

My mother covers my hair with a plastic bag to make the lice get so woozy they die.

I'm the one who's going to die, not the lice!

You're not going to die, you're going grow up and be a biiiiiig shot, and we're going to be so proud of you.

Mommy, does Hayna escape from her ghoul in the end?

The flabby woman is asleep on the cement, her arms her pillow. He says, I'm no soothsayer, and my mom still hasn't finished the story for me.

BRIWAT

He tells me that I don't love her. He takes a drag on his Casa cigarette, then goes on, "You just got used to having her around, that's all."

"So what is love, then?" I ask him. He gesticulates at length, eyes closed, as if he's about to reveal the secrets of atom formation. Then he feels around in his jacket pocket for his cigarettes and finally proclaims, in his ropy French, "Il n'y a pas une définition."

What he says might be true; perhaps I just got used to Miftaha, which, by the way, is her name. There's something sharp about her name: it makes me think of a needle. "Miftaha" is what my grandmother used to call needles. Her name also reminds me of the miftah, the key on a tin of sardines, and that's why I used to call her Fteeha instead. She'd get angry about that and tell me that when she was born her father slaughtered a fat, free-range rooster in her name, so I certainly didn't have any right to change it. I would tell her it was just an affection-ate nickname. That would make her smile, showing those wonky teeth she was trying in vain to conceal with her hand. But maybe I really was just used to her being around . . . I got used to finding her there every day after I got out of school (I'm a primary school teacher). I'd find her waiting for me. The first thing I'd do was scan for the black plastic bag: Did she have it or not? The black plastic bag was import-ant. I'd been imagining it throughout my eight-hour workday, my mouth watering, so I'd get a shock if she didn't bring it. Such a shock that I might cut our time together down from two hours to thirty minutes, on some pretext or other. And it seems she worked out what was going on, because eventually she stopped ever turning up without a plastic bag of chicken or lamb or prawn briwat in her hand. My favorite briwat are the prawn ones and the chicken ones. She lies, says she makes the briwat at home, especially for me. I know she buys them from Omi Mina, who sells them from a palm-frond basket she sets up near the Armil shoe shop in Maârif. Her voice sounds like a chicken squawking when she calls out: "Briwat, briiiwaaat . . ." One day I saw cockroaches going in and out of her palm-frond basket, so I swore I would never eat briwat again. But when I saw Fteeha, or in fact when I saw the black plastic bag, I tried to put that oath right out of my mind, telling myself that cockroaches actually aren't such bad bugs. I had once seen some Americans on TV eating a tray of roasted cockroaches with gusto. The sight of them made me switch off the set, saying to myself that even in times of total drought, famine, and bouhiouf, our forefathers didn't stoop to eating cockroaches. In the end, I came to the conclusion that the roaches in America must be a special kind and would definitely be high in vitamins.

I have, in fact, been used to her being around ever since childhood. We lived in the same karian, and at nap time, when we sensed that her father wanted to sleep, us kids would get together in front of his shack and shout, "Ew! Gross! What's Laarbi doing to that cat?" Because it was well known that Laarbi, Miftaha's father, had sex with cats. Cats mated and multiplied like crazy in our alley and never left Hell Hawker's shack. We used to call Laarbi "Hell Hawker" because he sold moonshine on the sly. Some of the older slakeet boys from the area took it even further and staged a grotesque wedding party. They got hold of a cat and tied it onto a white izaar sheet with some drops of blood and some sugar kawalibs on it. They put the whole lot onto a cart pulled by a scrawny, mangy horse, and the women of the karian followed along behind, ululating and shaking their bony butts. The crowd stopped in front of Hawker's shack door, dancing and throwing coins onto the bloodstained cloth. Hawker came out to see what was going on and one of them shouted, "Congratulations, Hawker! Wishing you bliss and babies!" Hawker calmly leaned over the coins on the blood-spattered cloth. He picked them up and went back into his shack, to the amazement of everyone present.

During all of this, Miftaha was looking over at us, apoplectic, and gesturing to me that she was going to slit my throat and hang me out to dry on the roof. So I put my middle finger up in her face and spat at her. Miftaha—or Fteeha—wasn't beautiful. Her teeth were crooked, and she had a bushy mustache, which was why we used to sometimes call her Abdelkader, making her so angry she'd throw stones at us ... But once we were grown up and I had discovered—I don't know how, or when—that I was in love with her, I told her when we were in Parc Murdoch, while I was eating chicken briwat, that her mustache didn't bother me but that in fact downy women were hot. She didn't know what being hot meant, but she seemed happy with that, and from then on, she took very good care of her mustache indeed.

But it's been a while now since I last found her waiting for me near the school with a black plastic bag in her hand. Or if she showed up it would be without the bag, and with a look of discomfort on her face. She generally looked uncomfortable anyway, so I really didn't pay her expression any mind; I was much more taken up with the disappearance of the bag and the briwat. One day—I don't remember exactly what day of the week it was, or the date, but it was five o'clock, so right when I got off work—we were sitting as usual in Parc Murdoch. I wanted to take the plastic bag from her, but she told me sharply, "Madame's done"—in other words, *the canteen is closed*—and then said that all she had in the bag were some sandals she'd bought for herself. I didn't like the way she spoke to me. Then without any preamble she informed me that someone had come forward wanting to marry her. I scrunched my toes tight inside my shoes to hold in a laugh that nearly escaped my mouth. She wanted to make me rush into marrying her, and all she could come up with to rope me in was this hackneyed story that could put you to sleep on your feet? Plus, who else apart from me on this whole earth would be foolish enough to settle for her? And because I was furious with her for buying the sandals instead of chicken or prawn briwat, I simply uttered the formulaic "Allah's bounty on that union," laughing silently to myself. I pictured her turning up the next day with her black plastic bag and claiming that she had rejected her suitor for my sake. I imagined how I would pretend to believe her, promising her that my problems were all to be solved soon—even though in truth I had none that needed solving. I'm paying for my apartment in easy installments, and there's a bed in it, a gas main, and some pans. I think that is what's required for a comfortable married life.

I remember that when Miftaha left that evening, she was muttering something about a lack of virility as she went, and about briwat. Now, I miss Miftaha so much that her name sounds musical to me, and I find there to be something beautiful and charming about her teeth. After school every day I rush out from class, hoping to find her waiting for me by the dried-fruit-and-nut stand with her black plastic bag, but in vain.

He says that I don't love her, that I just got used to having her around . . .

HOUSEFLY

He's wearing a shirt with a big checked pattern, black and white. It looks like a chessboard. Only the top half of his body is showing on her computer screen; she guesses he might perhaps be wearing yellow pants and tall winter boots, green socks and threadbare, orange knee-length underwear. She clamps her lips shut, but an audible snort of laughter escapes through her nose.

Boughattat70 messages her, In your picture your neck looks as tasty as a stick of jabaan kul obaan.

She laughs and writes back, Jabaan kul obaan! Remember the song the vendors used to sing?

Candies, eats and sees!

Squawking, squeaking kiddies!

Full sworn guarantees!

Blessed by Ouazzane Sufis!

Candies, eats and sees!

He replies, And I bet your tongue is as sweet as that faneed al-makana we all used to grind away on with our molars, back when we were kids.

—I don't like faneed al-makana. When I was a little girl, we traveled to a shrine to celebrate the mawsim festival there. It was for the marabout Sidi Rahal, actually. I bought some faneed al-makana. I stuck my head into that plastic bag and didn't pull it back out till I had scarfed down the very last piece. I didn't sleep at all that night: my butt was teeming with too many little worms. When I got sick of scratching that itch, I shouted out. My mother threatened to put hot chili pepper on it or tie me up inside the shrine. So after that I didn't shout anymore.

—Tell me about yourself.

—I don't feel like talking about myself.

—Are you a ghost?

—I'm a ghost, and you're Boughattat.

Her baby cries so she breastfeeds him and gurgles gentle sounds to soothe him. "There, there, gah gah gah, booboo baby." His fingers are tiny and pink. One day she's going to bite them off, or hug him so hard he suffocates. She wipes his bottom with Johnson's baby lotion, puts diapers on him, and doesn't hug him so that he won't die. When her husband comes home she'll serve him his dinner: tripe with turnip and red olives. He loves tripe. That's why she cooks it up in such big quantities, then puts it in the freezer to reheat when the need arises. In the freezer there's also enough bread to last a week, washed vegetables, and . . . all that stuff.

Jupiter1960 is now online.

She messages him, I've just performed the tagunja rain ritual.

—The rain is so late coming, and the land thirsts.

She licks her lips. Here comes her rain, it's gushing torrential.

Jupiter1960 writes, When I come to Casa, will you spend the night with me?

—Dream on! You're out of your mind.

—But let us dream, for a life without dreams, my friend, is loathsome. I'll bring a bottle of gin with me; it tastes good when it's blended with Schweppes tonic. Our encounter's going to be as hot as "summer in the southern cities," as the poet once said.

—And what else?

—When we meet, don't strangle your breasts in a bra . . . Let your hair hang free onto your shoulders, like in your photo. I want to line my eyes with the kohl of you: I'm a Bedouin, and my eyes are as big as my desire.

(Her husband says, "A woman's hair is shameful." His head is like an old piece of ivory, his beard is like a broom. Someday she's going to grab him by his beard, swing him around in the air three times, then throw him into the toilet and slosh a pail of water over him. She'll be shouting at him as she does it: "Your beard is shameful, your bald spot is shameful, your ass is shameful!")

Jupiter1960 writes, Do you want to make love?

(Her husband never asks. She lets him have her however he wants, whenever he wants, wherever he wants. Even if it's during the daytime in Ramadan. Ibn Qayyim al-Jawziyya says, "He who fears his testicles will burst, for him coitus is permitted during Ramadan." And she obeys her husband and obeys Ibn Qayyim, so that her husband's testicles don't burst open and she isn't barred from entering heaven.)

She grabs the keyboard and hammers out, Does love taste different when it's made over the internet?

—Of course it does. And it's as delicious as our mothers' couscous.

(She licks her lips. On Friday she's going to her mother's place to eat couscous made with gueddid. Her husband will go with her, of course, and she'll wear her black clothes, as usual, looking like some tent on legs—her siblings call her "the Ninja." The tent stifles her, her husband stifles her, and Jupiter1960 is writing to her now, A woman isn't just a body.)

She writes to him, When we meet we'll go to the sea. We'll watch the seagulls alighting and we'll eat ice cream . . .

—I'll read Juwaida's "Poem of the Seagulls" to you.

—I'll gift the sea my body, and I'll tell it, "Come to me!"

—Gift your body to me and say that to me, and you'll see that I won't be like Yusuf and shun you.

—You're crazy.

—When we sneak into my friend's room, I'll read you a poem by Rimbaud. We'll roll a couple of cigarettes and smoke them, and drink a glass or two of gin. I'll fan the flames of you until your fires roar, I'll awaken those timeless volcanoes slumbering deep inside you. I'm a Zoroastrian lover: I worship fire.

(She recalls Rimbaud, Nass El Ghiwane, university . . . she was pushing forty before she got married.)

—My my, with all this milk on offer I'll never need to buy a cow.

The clock on the wall strikes eight. In half an hour her husband will be home. Eight thirty always ushers in a heart-shrinking gloom. She shuts down Messenger and puts everything back in its place. When her husband arrives he'll wolf down his plate of tripe, pray the evening prayer, shut his office door, and be alone with his computer.

A housefly buzzes near her ear. It hovers over her baby's face. He wakes ... "Shhhh" ... She swats the fly away. Her baby goes back to sleep. Her husband always says, "If I found out a male fly had gotten into my house, I'd kill it."

DEATH

For all that pure, spilled blood

I switch on the TV with the remote control, and the presenter smiles, revealing her shiny white teeth. How does she keep them so white?

—and Israel has attacked Gaza City in retaliation for the killing of two Israeli soldiers.

Her smile widens. She's wearing green contact lenses today, the exact same shade as her tight green dress. Green doesn't suit her . . . The dress shows off her perfectly round breasts.

"Help me set the table."

"Lamb would've been plenty. Why did you fry up chicken as well?"

Decaying corpses—

I stick my knife and fork into a piece of meat and gobble it up enthusiastically.

—*decapitated heads*—

"Mmmm, well done. The meat is delicious," says my husband.

The presenter is trying to put on a sad face . . . It doesn't suit her.

Mothers crying—

"Look at her dress, it's très belle."

—*misery, poverty*—

"I want a glass of Tang."

—*screaming*—

I pour the juice for my daughter.

—*blood-soaked asphalt*—

"Coca-Cola is better, it helps digestion."

"But it causes gas."

And Israel is using weapons and bombs that are banned internationally—

"Maman, look! I'm dancing like Nancy Ajram."

The little girl writhes around, singing, "*Ah wa nos, bos bos bos.*"

I applaud her. She's exactly like I was at her age.

"God keep you safe, my beautiful girls," says my husband.

My little boy gets jealous, jumps off his chair. "I'm better than her at singing!"

He balls his fist as if holding a mic:

Why don't you come to me, kitty cat,

I bought you some shisha and chocolate,

But you ask me for a suit and a little hat!"

I'm laughing so much there are tears in my eyes.

"Don't speak with your mouth full, mon petit."

"But *you're* talking, toi et Maman!"

"Maman and I are talking about important things."

My little boy goes quiet, and so does my little girl.

In Iraq forty-two civilians have been killed, three of them children, and fifteen others injured, seven of whom are in critical condition, after a bomb was dropped—

"On Saturday night let's go to Balcon 33. There'll be an American belly dancer performing!"

"No, there's a big match on Saturday—al-Raja are playing Widad—and I'll get home from the stadium exhausted. Mind you, if Widad win, we can go wherever you want."

"One day football's going to be the death of you."

"I know, right? A real man is someone who dies for his country, or his family, or for Widad."

"Reds forever! Reds, Reds, Reds! Can I come with you to the match?" my son asks happily.

"If you finish memorizing your schoolwork, then yes, we'll go."

"I did all the exercises, I've just got history left. I couldn't memorize everything, it's too hard!"

"Look, I'll tell you exactly how it works: history is easy. It's just the same lessons repeating themselves over and over."

The presenter is still talking. Bright red lipstick doesn't suit her . . . It makes her mouth seem too big for her face.

Two ferries full of tourists will depart today for Spain—

—the sudden war on Lebanon—

—and Israel has refused—

—until—

—the departure of the tourists.

"Wake me in an hour, I'm dead tired," says my husband, then he stretches out in front of the television . . .

TRANSLATOR'S NOTE

Malika Moustadraf (1969–2006) lived, worked, and died in the major port city of Casablanca, on the Atlantic west coast of Morocco. She published just one novel, a single short story collection, one other short story, and a few articles during her short life. After her death, three more short stories were published in a literary magazine. The short story collection and the four subsequent stories are what make up *Blood Feast*, the first ever full-length translation of her work. This slim volume is but a snapshot of a gifted maverick writer in her ascendancy, creatively going from strength to strength even as her health deteriorated during the final weeks before her death. Had her life not been tragically cut short, Moustadraf would undoubtedly have gone on to reach great artistic heights. In 2022 she would have been just fifty-three, eight years older than me. I would have certainly visited her in Casablanca over these last six years since I've been reading and translating her work, and would have gotten to know her. We would have spent time hanging out in her favorite café, working through the innumerable fascinating linguistic and cultural questions any serious literary translation project generates. Perhaps we would have enjoyed ranting to each other about the patriarchy, exchanging music, making each other laugh? And surely, by now, she would have become more widely respected and less persecuted for her feminist activist sensibility than she was at the turn of the millennium. But she did die in 2006, and so this modest oeuvre is all we have—the culmination of her life's work, all but lost to the world over the last fifteen years since her untimely death.

Moustadraf's first work was the novel *Wounds of the Soul and the Body* (*Jirah al-ruh wa-l-jasad*), which she self-published in 1999. As important as this debut was in terms of establishing her as a talented and radical voice, it was also very much the work of a beginner, an outsider artist. According to some sources, Moustadraf was still in her teens when she wrote *Wounds*, working on it in secret in the bathroom of her family home. Nevertheless, it demonstrated an early unpolished version of what was to become Moustadraf's signature style: an unflinching look at the worst traumas of the female experience in patriarchal society, shot through with wit, wordplay, and razor-sharp political commentary. In addition to centering the survivor protagonist's first-person account of multiple childhood sexual assaults, a central theme of that first book is sex work and the extent to which it props up the Moroccan domestic economy and underpins working-class urban family life. *Wounds* also poignantly examines women's homoemotional bonding in the context of extreme gendered oppression, and the impossibility of equitable heterosexuality, with a strong yet delicate and understated queer sensibility.

The short story collection she went on to write after publishing *Wounds*, all translated here in *Blood Feast*, very much built on that foundation, moving into uncharted territory in terms of both form and content. Professionally, she was taken seriously at last—the collection, titled *Trente-Six*, impressed the prestigious Moroccan Short Story Research Group[1] so much that the authors and academics involved in the organization banded together to pay her publishing costs. Stylistically, the stories in *Trente-Six* demonstrate a new proficiency and confidence: the writing is more carefully thought out and reworked than Moustadraf's previous material, and yet also more playful. Moustadraf reaches a new level of linguistic experimentation—especially in the last four stories she wrote, which conclude *Blood Feast*—featuring a wider use of Derija and realist linguistic hybridity, and developing what was becoming her signature "refragmented memory" device,[2] playing with temporal modes and layered flashbacks. She seems much freer in these stories than she was in her novel, roaming through a range of topics, voices, settings, and points of focus—always keeping it "rebel realist"[3] and feminist. In the *Trente-Six* stories, Moustadraf enjoys a newfound complexity: she likes her characters multilayered, contradictory, flawed, wounded, and human; for example, we encounter homophobia and misogyny in characters for whom we are simultaneously being moved to compassion. The writer has come of age and is blossoming in the approval of her literary peers—as well as weathering the inevitable misogynistic backlash.

Moustadraf had, in fact, intended to write a second novel, but her deteriorating health meant the work instead became a short story collection, composed in between dialysis sessions as her strength allowed. Interviewed by the young Moroccan poet Mouna Ouafik just after *Trente-Six* was published in 2004, Moustadraf sounded like she felt her major life's work was still ahead of her, and talked of saving her full confrontation with society for later:

> It's not easy to stand naked while everyone looks on, seeing you in your nudity. But one day I really *am* going to get naked, right down to the last fig leaf. What violations and crimes I've been the victim of, and still am! I will try to rip off some masks, so that everyone can see just how ugly our faces look without them on. But for now, I'll settle for biting my tongue. I'm staying silent, so that I don't waste my energy with too much talking, because when the time comes for the explosion, I want it to be an earthshaking

volcanic eruption. . . . I want it to be a slap in the face for all those politicians and pimps who claim to be so virtuous and pure . . . the ones who turn our dreams into frustrations and sorrows.[4]

When she died, Moustadraf was in the early stages of coauthoring a novel with Palestinian poet and academic Aida Nasrallah.[5] "Death," the final story in *Blood Feast*, was the last story Moustadraf ever completed, as far as we know. The biggest question about any artist who dies young—especially poignant given the exponential stylistic development so clearly underway in her last four stories—is, What would she have gone on to write had she survived?

One of the conventions of translators' notes is to recount something of the original author's biography, especially if the author is dead, a woman, an outspoken feminist rebel, a Muslim, or all of the above, as is the case here. But what relevance does the true-life story of Malika Moustadraf really have to the works of fiction you hold in your hands? The biographies of women writers from the global South are very often expected to inform and interweave with their fiction. It is much harder for these writers to have their writing received as feats of pure imagination than it is for others, especially white cis male writers. Marilyn Booth has explored this noted phenomenon in the specific context of arabophone Muslim women writers in her useful work on memoir fixation and Orientalist ethnographicisim,[6] and it was something that Moustadraf herself was only too aware of. Throughout her life as a published author, Moustadraf was bombarded with speculation and accusation around the extent to which her writing was based on her own experience, something she found very intrusive, and which negatively impacted her quality of life and ultimately contributed to her death. In that same 2004 interview by Mouna Ouafik, soon after *Trente-Six* was published, she said, "The thing that really bothers me is when other people consider what I've written to be autobiography. Why can't they acknowledge that women [like men] also have a broad imagination?!"[7]

The issue is even more sensitive in our context,

since the material that was seen as autobiographical in Moustadraf's novel was a first-person account of surviving serial child sexual abuse. In the late 1990s and early 2000s in Morocco, the possibility that this was not fiction—and even the simple act of writing such stories at all—was vehemently condemned by some sections of society and public life. The novel's central topics of rape and sex work were seen as inherently shameful—and so, by extension, was the author herself. As Moustadraf commented to Ouafik in the same interview, "Women have always been, and still are, accused of being the true protagonists of what they write. Why are women prosecuted for what they write, unlike men? Quite simply, because we live in a patriarchal society."[8]

The speculation and controversy over whether the accounts of child sexual abuse were rooted in her own experience continued after her death. Her own statements on record as to if and to what extent her novel was based on her own life are (perhaps understandably) somewhat contradictory, and this is not the place to make a judgment call on that issue. What is clear is that Moustadraf was not living and writing in a context in which she would have felt safe to tell a survivor's story, had she even wanted to. Rather than giving definitive testimony one way or the other as to her own childhood experiences, she wanted her work to speak for itself, and to act on her behalf. As she put it to Ouafik, "I shoot down some of those who wielded their unjust authority over me, tyrannized and oppressed me, with bullets from my pen—and I inter them between the pages of a book."[9]

Has the world changed enough since 2006 that Moustadraf would be sharing more about her life, were she still alive? What would she want me to say on her behalf? The translator of a dead author faces many such unanswerable questions. The difficulty is compounded, in our current context, by the urge to believe survivors, and to honor that trauma she hinted at. But ultimately, I feel it's a valid choice to focus instead on honoring the raging courage of her literary activism and cherishing the smart, sassy art she made around the central traumas of the patriarchal world, rather than on whether or not these things actually happened to her. In this way, we allow for the possibility, as Moustadraf herself affirmed, that women writers have a fertile imagination.

Even without making a call on the issues above, sketching an outline of Moustadraf's brief and troubled life is not an easy task, due to the dearth and inaccuracy of available sources. This lack of a coherent record seems to be part of a certain abandonment of her legacy, despite the high regard in which her work was and is still held by many Moroccan literary folk, artists, academics, and critics. As a self-styled rebel realist woman writer, she was too much for many people to handle. Her work was only ever published within Morocco, and when she died in 2006, her two books had already fallen out of print. Her death generated various media tributes, which sparked a new wave of interest in her work and led to all remaining copies of her books, new and used, being snapped up by an engaged public. This was also when her final three stories were published for the first time, by the literary magazine *QS*—yet no one republished her two books. A book of scholarly and hagiographic articles on Moustadraf and her work was published in Arabic in 2017,[10] featuring a few of her stories. But her books remained out of print until I introduced her oeuvre to an Egyptian publishing house known for its confrontational and feminist work, and they published new editions of both *Wounds* and *Trente-Six* in 2020.[11]

I first came across Moustadraf's work in 2016, when fellow translator Emma Ramadan asked me to translate "Delusion" for a Words Without Borders feature on Moroccan writers. Moustadraf had been recommended to Ramadan by writer and curator Omar Berrada. Instantly smitten with Moustadraf's work, I set out to find more of it, but I soon discovered that copies of this cult figure's books were such rare commodities that fans were circulating low-grade scans of her work via word of mouth.[12] So I, too, worked from those scans, and as I continued researching Moustadraf's extraordinary life and work over the ensuing years, and publishing my translations of a few of her stories,[13] I became a point of contact for this PDF traffic and would regularly be approached by strangers seeking to read her work. I was only eventually able to get a hard copy of *Trente-Six* due to the immense generosity of her original publisher, Abdelmajid Jahfa, who gifted me his personal copy. A couple of her stories had appeared in French and English here and there over the last decade before I began to translate her, but *Blood Feast* is the first full-length work of hers published in translation in any language.

Given the near extinction of her work, it is perhaps not surprising that most of the scant information about her life available online consists of repeated (and often distorted) versions of just a few original source pieces. There are frequent inaccuracies and anomalies, not least in the meager trickle of references to her in English over the years, several of which have her year of birth and death wrong. Many aspects of her story are a contested narrative. Accounts of her life made to me personally by her friends and associates often contradict one another, and given that her life story is a tragedy, it's understandably a very charged topic for those who are still grieving her loss, just fifteen years after her death.

In many ways, the book you're holding (and the 2020 Arabic reissues) represents the culmination of a long project of literary recovery of a foundational body of feminist work that had all but disappeared; as part of that effort, I've compiled a sketch of what we know of her life, based as much as possible on her own words in the few extant published interviews.

So, who was Malika Moustadraf?

She was a feminist literary activist focused on sexuality, patriarchy, disability, illness, class, and women's rights. Her friends remember her as having an intense and innate feminist rage, a keen eye for the ridiculous, and a ringing, infectious laugh—all of which sing out in her work. She loved music and was great friends with Nass el-Ghiwane founder Larbi Batma. She loved the color blue. She read widely, and was fascinated by the French "carnal artist" ORLAN. She lived with her extended family in the central Casablanca neighborhood of Maârif. She was very close to her young nephew, Issam, to whom *Trente-Six* was dedicated. In the 2004 interview with Ouafik, she talked of always spending her Saturdays with the boy, and feeling transported to a happy childhood state with him.

As an outsider, it's problematic to talk about writers as "the only" or "the first"; those lazy, absolutist claims are made all too often, and erase nuance and multiplicity. There have always been feminist artists everywhere. But at the same time, it is important to acknowledge Moustadraf's vanguard status: she was ahead of her time by just a few years—the contemporary Moroccan feminist artists and activists working on gender and sexuality now are just a generation (or less) younger than her.[14] Had she lived, she surely would have been engaged with this vibrant scene. There are also two concrete firsts for Arabic literature in this collection as far as I can establish: "Head Lice" and "Housefly" feature what are probably the first ever published literary depictions of cybersex in Arabic, portraying a way of relating that would have seemed extraordinarily unfamiliar, even futuristic, to readers at that time. And in a more major potential first for modern Arabic literary fiction, "Just Different" features an intersex and/or trans protagonist. (It doesn't seem to me that Moustadraf is spelling out, in this text, whether the protagonist—assigned male at birth and violently misgendered throughout their life—is intersex, or trans, or both. Various readings are possible.)[15] Crucially, this is an ambitious and nuanced portrait, not only of the character but of the various dynamics in which they are engaged, including difficult medical scenes—interwoven with folkloric references and complex puns based on grammatical terms. And as in her earlier work, Moustadraf is inviting us to engage sympathetically with a sex worker. Marché Centrale, where the protagonist of that story solicits, is not far from where Malika lived, and she would likely have observed gender nonconforming sex workers there.

Whatever the exact details of Moustadraf's experience as a child, there had certainly been some attempts made to silence her at a young age: she had been taught it was shameful to write about the topics she gravitated toward. And as an adult, she felt that society was ordering her to keep quiet, and that there was one set of rules for male writers and another for women. She told Ouafik, "Men can say anything and everything, it's all accepted. But if a woman expresses what *she's* burning to say, then shame on her, she's got no manners. We're accustomed to men saying everything on behalf of women. They want us to just be pretty and keep quiet!"[16]

Moustadraf's friend Aida Nasrallah also recounts in her memoir that a prominent male intellectual told Moustadraf that she "deserved" her illness for writing the way she did.[17] Moustadraf reportedly suffered great distress over this. But none of this fully silenced her in the end—the things she observed in society that made her the angriest continued to come out in her writing throughout her life.

Moustadraf's work was completed in the context of multiple oppressions in both the private and public spheres, and all while ill. Sources differ on exactly when she developed kidney disease and began dialysis, but we know it was sometime in her teens. She was unable to complete her university studies because of her condition. It seems creative writing was simultaneously her equivalent of an academic discipline, her life's passion, and her mental health survival strategy: "For me, writing is a kind of drug: it keeps me from thinking about the pain, because if I kept on thinking about all the pain and the health problems I'm suffering from, then in all honesty I would go mad, or commit suicide. So writing is a kind of sedative for the pain I live with. It allows me to submerge myself in other worlds and other characters."[18]

As anyone living with chronic illness knows, however, what contributes to mental survival doesn't necessarily aid the physical condition. It's a sad irony that while her dedication to her art clearly improved her mental health, it also contributed to her physical deterioration: her condition was permanently exacerbated when she skipped doses of essential anemia and calcium medication in order to cover the costs of publishing her first book. There is a story that is frequently told about Moustadraf having been nurtured and supported in her work by her neighbor, the canonical Moroccan writer Mohamed Zafzaf, who is said to have been something of a literary godfather figure to her (the implication being, by extension, that he taught her how to write). In an interview with Abdelali Barakat in 2003, however, Moustadraf recalled how when she approached Zafzaf in 1996 for advice on how to get her novel published as an unknown writer, he refused to read or discuss her manuscript, and in what sounds like a scene from one of her stories, hid it under his bed.[19] After two years of trying to persuade him to engage with her work or recommend publishers she might approach, she eventually gave up and covered the costs of self-publishing the book the only way she could, by cutting back on her meds.[20] When asked in 2004 if she regretted having done this, since it had led to her becoming reliant on crutches to walk, she said, "Yes, I bitterly regret it! If I'd known that that craziness would end up with me on crutches, I never would have done it."[21]

Her health had also been impacted by the after-effects of a suicide attempt: "Once, feeling defeated, I resolved to kill myself: I swallowed a quantity of pills, but death spat me back out—back to life, to live in a body even more burnt out and exhausted than ever. As you can see, life is insistent with me."[22]

In the latter years of her life, Moustadraf was severely ill, with very restricted mobility and extremely debilitating symptoms. She was essentially housebound, only leaving her home for hospital trips. But this final period of her life coincided with the early days of the internet, a development which provided her a lifeline with the outside world, allowing her to meet and converse at length with new people and old friends. She was especially keen on debating with other writers. She was an early adopter of MSN Messenger, one of the first online chat platforms, using it for long, late-night conversations with her friends in Palestine, Saudi Arabia, and elsewhere—and as noted earlier, exploring this new technology in her final works of fiction.

Engaged in a protracted and ultimately futile struggle to obtain life-saving treatment either at home or abroad, she lived in close proximity to death for the last several years of her life. A kidney transplant from her sister Karima back in 1990 had been unsuccessful, as Moustadraf mentions in the poignant dedication to the story "Blood Feast." She was campaigning to be able to make another transplant attempt with a new donor, and meanwhile becoming more and more ill as time passed. Other patients died during dialysis sessions in the ward she regularly attended, and friends of hers died awaiting treatment. Two years before Moustadraf herself died, she suggested that the struggle to obtain the treatment she needed was already more than she could bear: "Death no longer scares me. I consider it a transitional phase from one world to another, perhaps even to a better one. If over there on the other shore there is no hospital, nor any horrible people denying you of your right to treatment, well, that would be enough."[23] In her memoir, Aida Nasrallah describes the profound emotional distress Moustadraf suffered in private at receiving hate mail calling her a beggar.[24] Publicly Moustadraf raged at the system: "Begging for treatment in my own country?! It's shameful for treatment to become a luxury not everyone is allowed to access!"[25]

In September 2006, at the age of thirty-seven, Moustadraf eventually died of complications related to chronic kidney disease, due to lack of access to the surgery she needed. It's a complex and very dark tale involving Fortress Europe (she was denied a Schengen visa at a crucial point, for travel to Germany for surgery there), her persecution by some sections of the Moroccan intellectual elite who declined to lobby for her being treated, and the nature of the corrupt and crumbling semiprivatized health-care system in her homeland, among other factors. Without going any further into all of those distressing details, she could and should have lived much longer.

However, she did also have some very passionate supporters during the last desperate phase of her life, among them Moroccan literary superstar Ahmed Bouzfour, who refused the Moroccan state literary prize he was awarded in 2004 in protest over (among other issues) Moustadraf not being granted treatment, stating, "I would feel ashamed to take this prize from my sister Malika Moustadraf, who is dying before our very eyes while we remain silent."[26] There was also a fundraiser organized on her behalf by the Saudi Arabian newspaper *Al-Riyadh* that raised $50,000 for her medical costs—funds that were sadly never able to be used as planned.[27] At points in her struggle, Médecins Sans Frontières was involved, and she even had a correspondence with the UK's Prince Charles. But needless to say, it all was in vain.

Blocked from accessing the treatment she needed and facing the increasingly likely prospect of her death, Moustadraf repeated to Ouafik, "Death doesn't scare me anymore. I've been sentenced to death by the doctors twice already. Whenever I start a dialysis session, I never know if I'll be going home on my feet or on my back. But what does truly scare me is my figurative death: being marginalized, under siege, excluded. That's real death!"[28]

The central tragedy is that Moustadraf's life could have been saved, and was not. There's no way to make up for that. But it is my hope that her work coming back into print in Arabic and appearing for the first time in English is just the beginning of a long-overdue literary resurrection of Malika Moustadraf, and thereby goes at least some way toward addressing the fear of erasure she expressed so poignantly.

Now that I've told you something of who the author of these stories was, what about the worlds she created in them? In any translation (in any text, perhaps), there are inevitably a host of references that will be lost on many readers. Unfamiliar words or proper names can, of course, be researched by those readers inclined to take that approach, and we have created a glossary for this English edition for those who enjoy that particular mode. Some of the most interesting extratextual material alive in Moustadraf's work, however, doesn't hinge on a single key word, and so I feel it is worth flagging a few of the myriad examples of the depths beneath the surface of her work. For the explanations that follow, I want to express my deepest gratitude to my friends in Morocco, whose generosity and hospitality (linguistic, translational, intellectual, and practical, whether in person or remote) seem to know no bounds. All errors and misunderstandings, however, are mine alone, as the saying goes.

Idiomatic Moroccan expressions are frequent in Moustadraf's writing, many of which will be easily understandable, in context, to the anglophone reader of my translation. Others are more oblique, or only reveal part of their meaning to the unfamiliar reader. In "Just Different," for example, one might wonder why the protagonist's father objects so strongly to their standing in a certain position, and summons up a popular expression to illustrate his point: "'Hands behind him, carrying the devil on his back'—that was what he used to say to me if he caught me with my hands behind my back" (22). There are two main issues here, both revolving around emasculation: One is that women traditionally carry children on their backs, but men do not, so to have one's hands behind one's back implies bearing a child, supposedly a uniquely feminine posture. The other aspect is that the back itself is associated with sex in Moroccan popular culture and, combined with the devil, the suggestion is of a risk of anal penetration—another emasculating act, in the mind of this character's father.

In "Raving," the protagonist uses a popular folk saying when she wonders about her lover: "Is it true he has an extra rib?" (61). This is a reference to Saharwi men (from Western Sahara) being seen in a certain popular imagination as such big macho men that they actually possess an extra rib. In "Housefly," the protagonist awaits her favorite online date, and chats to another male user in the meantime. When he pays her trite compliments based on childhood candies, she weirds it up by recounting a dark childhood memory of giving herself threadworms from gorging on some dirty street candy. The phrase "having worms" in Moroccan slang, however, means feeling horny, so the translation loss here is huge.

In "A Woman in Love, a Woman Defeated," the new bride hears a popular expression from the groom about the need for a husband to assert his authority from the get go: "The first thing he did was slap me and say, 'The cat dies on day one,' and I knew that, in this context, I was the cat" (54). Earlier in the story, when trying to convince her mother that she's made the right choice of prospective husband, she quotes an expression her mother frequently uses back at her: *"But Mom, aren't you are always saying, 'A covered head is better than a bare head'"* (53). The idea here is that getting married is akin to getting dressed, to being decent—it's more halal for a woman to be married than not.

There are a range of direct and indirect references to Islamic concepts such as this in

Moustadraf's work that might elude the reader not usually exposed to much Muslim culture, or might seem more formal and overtly religious than they do in their original context. When the same love-lorn protagonist longs for her mother to soothe her to sleep with the words *"Allah, Allah . . . Mohammed is Allah's messenger"* (52), the connotation is of Sufi chants, used to soothe and comfort, a form of spiritual poetry with rhythm used in Gnawa, and also familiar to children as a lullaby. During the erotic online conversation in "Housefly," the woman protagonist makes a single-phrase allusion to Surah Yusuf (also known in English as Joseph, depending on the translation), a Surah dealing with physical beauty, carnal desire, seduction, and self-restraint. When she says, "I'll gift the sea my body, and I'll tell it, 'Come to me!'" (108), she is quoting ayah 23: "The woman in whose house he dwelt sought to seduce him and shut firm the doors upon them. She said: 'Come to me!' He said: 'God forbid!'"[29] Her internet lover immediately picks up on the reference and tells her to gift her body to him instead of the sea, reassuring her he "won't be like Yusuf, and shun you" (108). Another instance of lovers quoting Islamic text while chatting online occurs in "Head Lice." The imprisoned woman protagonist recalls paraphrasing a well-known hadith to lend strength to her argument: "He who can't afford to marry, let him fast from the carnal feast" (91). This hadith is narrated in Sahih al-Bukhari as: "O young people! Whoever among you is able to marry, should marry, and whoever is not able to marry, is recommended to fast, as fasting diminishes his sexual urge."[30]

In "Just Different," the protagonist's father hears the word *pilot* as containing the word *Lot*, the name of the Quranic and Biblical figure. "He frowned, clearly thinking about something weighty, and kept repeating, "*Lot . . . pee-Lot*" (23). Although there is a rich array of interpretations of the story of Sodom and Gomorrah, and its status as a holy proscription of same-sex desire is strongly contested, the popular interpretation of Lot's role has led to his name forming a common pejorative term for homosexual in Arabic, "Loti." Using Lot as a standalone proper name, the father is accusing his child of what he sees as sinful sexual deviance, hence the outburst that follows this rumination.

Other folk cultural references in the collection include the sampling in "Head Lice" of parts of the well-known folk tale Hayna and the Ghoul, loosely akin to Rapunzel in that it centers the power of physical beauty and hair. In "A Woman in Love, a Woman Defeated," the protagonist reminisces on a popular children's chant: "Ashtatata, pour, pour, pour, pour your rain down" (51). This familiar ditty, often sung at the start of the rainy season by children in contemporary Moroccan urban life, is originally related to an ancient Amazigh ritual for times of drought. Performed in rural areas, the ritual involves building an effigy of the rain's betrothed. There is then a procession to every local water source by the young girls of the community while the older men sing long songs to entice the rain.

There are multiple folk cultural references in the story "Briwat." Reading it in a context such as Britain, where I'm from—a place where about a quarter of all households nationally include a feline pet—the reader might not pick up on the intensity of the domestic transgression Hell Hawker represents. Like "The Ruse," this story is set in a karian: an impoverished neighborhood of unregulated improvised residential structures, lacking in infrastructure, and often inhabited by recent migrants to the city from rural areas. Obviously in these conditions most people can't spare food for pets, so taboos around them flourish. Hell Hawker is being accused of bestiality, a universal taboo, but there's more going on here: cats are associated with devils and djinns in Moroccan popular culture, thought to live in haunted places. This adds another layer to Miftaha's marginalized status as his child—living with cats is almost satanic, so she's suffering under that label. The reality of the situation Moustadraf alludes to is that this widower is selling moonshine to make ends meet, enough to make him a pariah, someone other parents want to keep their children away from— so the bestiality myths spring from there, to make excluding him from the community easier. The mock wedding party staged to taunt Hell Hawker (and to provide some entertainment in a neighborhood in which leisure activity options are extremely limited) is one of only very few instances in which I inserted a "stealth gloss" into the translated text: the phrase "staged a grotesque wedding party" (98) does not appear in the original. To a reader familiar with Moroccan wedding culture, there would be no need to spell it out, since it would be absolutely clear from the horse-drawn cart, the izaar, the kawalibs (see glossary), the ululating, and the celebratory chants that this was a parody of a wedding between Hell Hawker and his cats. There are also clues within this scene to certain specifics of karian culture: the wedding cart on which the groom would tradition-ally bring the bridal gifts and money to the bride's house is "pulled by a scrawny, mangy horse" (98)—it seems these new arrivals to the urban karian from the countryside still have some animals with them, not in use now in the city, too old to really work anymore.

There is a rich thread of material around the world of djinn and magic running through Moustadraf's work, intertwined with references to Gnawa ritual practices (see multiple glos-sary entries). Some of these references are in the foreground of the action, as in "A Woman in Love, a Woman Defeated," in which the protagonist seeks the help of a soothsayer to sort out her love life, and the idea of possession by a djinn is spelled out. Other references are more oblique, such as when the soothsayer "demands submission" (55) during one of the protagonist's consultations with her: she's using a formulaic phrase for when someone is believed to have djinns possessing them—the idea being that until they are exorcised, the demons must be obeyed rather than resisted or harmed, so that they don't harm their host. In other stories, the supernatural is in the background, as in "Thirty-Six," when the girl is disturbed by a picture of "a big monkey wrapping toilet paper around his huge, hairy body, his jaw hanging open idiotically to reveal rusty teeth the size of fava beans" (34). She's not just cringing at a late twentieth-century viral image familiar to many anglophone readers, she's seeing an animal so associated with djinns in popular culture that it is essentially a monster to her, displayed on the wall of her home. In "The Ruse," the bride's mother and aunt are concerned with the concrete physical reality at the center of the story—the bride's hymen—but we learn from their conversational asides that witchcraft is part of these women's daily lives. A specific impotence curse, thiqaaf (see glossary), is mentioned in passing, and the idea that the "evil eye of envy" (1) has real power to derail a wedding is taken for granted. The two women are particularly concerned about Aicha the Slaughtered because of her unibrow, a facial feature commonly used in early depictions of evil in Moroccan culture. But none of this is magical realism, and these are ordinary, contemporary, urban lives. It's worth noting that Moustadraf is by no means implying that everyone in her society believes in these things or worries about them, as plenty of her characters clearly do not. But the supernatural is a key cultural element she interweaves into several of her narratives with varying degrees of intensity.

Given all that she lived through, it's not surprising that Malika Moustadraf doubted the power (or even the point) of writing. Sounding jaded in her

2004 interview with Ouafik, she said, "There was a time when I actually thought, in my delusion, that writing was capable of changing something."[31] Her outspoken feminist literary activism clearly did not seem to have the effect she had once dreamed of. And, as she was already suspecting by then that it would, her writing contributed to her death, via the furious backlash it provoked in some quarters, and how that affected her access to life-saving treatment. There's no way to make that reality ever feel just, and no way to make up for the loss of her. But what about the mysterious afterlife of a dead writer's work? Her words are back in print in Arabic now, being read by new readers. Her work is also arriving in another language, and perhaps traveling on from here to yet more languages, to be read in places far from Casablanca. What might her words spark in her new readers? Like Moustadraf, I am also prone to doubting the power of writing. But knowing that reading can change lives (and has changed mine), here I am. Above all, *Blood Feast* is my own act of friendship and of hospitality, to Malika, the dear friend I never had the chance to meet. I hope you

will make her welcome too, and enjoy her company
on the page as much as I have.

—Alice Guthrie
Granada, Spain
October 2021

NOTES

1. Based at the Casablanca University Hassan II, the Moroccan Short Story Research Group has been an important publisher of original literary works, translations, and the literary journal *QS*. They also hold regular workshops.
2. The term *refragmented memory* was coined by the artist Noureddine Ezarraf, whose thinking around Moustadraf's work has been invaluable to my understanding and rendering of her writing.
3. Moustadraf apparently repeatedly used this phrase, a take on the more familiar "magical realist," in conversation and private correspondence as quoted by Aida Nasrallah and others.
4. Malika Moustadraf, interview by Mouna Ouafik, published on Mohamed Aslim's cultural website on July 24, 2004, http://aslimnet.free.fr/div/malika2.htm. All quotes from this and other interviews are my own translations.

   Ouafik and another young writer friend who were passionate about "literature from the margins" had the presence of mind to arrange and conduct this remarkable interview with Moustadraf before she died, which is one of the main extant sources of the writer discussing her life and work. On its publication in summer 2004, the interview was very widely shared and read around the arabophone world.

5. Aida Nasrallah quotes several short extracts from the material they were developing together in her poetic and political travelogue and memoir of her relationship with Moustadraf and others. See Aida Nasrallah, *Ayyami ma'Malika* [My days with Malika] (Tangiers, Morocco: Edition Slaiki, 2019).

6. See, for example, Marilyn Booth, "'The Muslim Woman' as Celebrity Author and the Politics of Translating Arabic: Girls of Riyadh Go on the Road," *Journal of Middle East Women's Studies* 6, no. 3 (Fall 2010): 149–82.

7. Moustadraf, interview by Ouafik, 2004.

8. Moustadraf, interview by Ouafik, 2004.

9. Moustadraf, interview by Ouafik, 2004.

10. *Malika Mustazraf farashat al-sard al-maghribi* [Malika Moustadraf, the butterfly of Moroccan prose] (Fes, Morocco: Editions Approches, 2017).

11. AlRabie Publications' edition of *Trente-Six* is an expanded version of the original collection, as (like *Blood Feast*) it includes the four extra stories originally published in *QS* magazine. It's essentially a complete short stories volume but published under the same name as the older, shorter collection. The texts have been edited in a slightly slapdash way by the new publisher, so Moustadraf purists or scholars would be advised to consult the originals, but the stories are largely unchanged and back in circulation, which is a positive step.

12. Aida Nasrallah argues that Moustadraf always had a bigger readership online than in print, due to the early efforts made by the Moroccan literary site Douroub (no longer

in existence) to feature her work, and later to the ubiquity of pirating in Arabic literature and the issues with book distribution across the region. It's outside the scope of this piece to try to assess this, but there is anecdotal evidence that Moustadraf was read in Arabic outside Morocco, and it seems likely this would have occurred mostly online.

13. "Delusion" was published by Words Without Borders in March 2016, and "Just Different" was published by *The Common* in April 2016.

14. Leïla Slimani and Zainab Fasiki are two obvious examples of Moroccan feminist artists who have obtained widespread and mainstream visibility in recent years. Aside from these famous names, there is a diverse wealth of Moroccan feminist activists and artists (or artivists), including queer and trans feminists, active today.

15. Since premodern Arabic literature is a vast treasure trove of gender and sexual diversity, I'm not making any claims about that period, just the last hundred years or so. I would be very interested to hear from anyone who has a modern Arabic literary reference for a nuanced and sympathetic portrait of an intersex or gender nonconforming person predating Moustadraf's work.

16. Moustadraf, interview by Ouafik, 2004.

17. Nasrallah, *Ayyami maʿ Malika* [My days with Malika], 116.

18. Malika Moustadraf, interview by Abdelhaq Ben Rahmoun, *Azzaman* newspaper, issue 1691, December 22, 2003.

19. Abdelali Barakat's 2003 interview for the newspaper *Bayane al Yaoume* was republished in a tribute to Moustadraf on the occasion of the thirteenth anniversary of her death, in September 2018. Abdelali Barakat, "Commemorating the thirteenth anniversary of the death of the Moroccan writer

Malika Moustadraf" [al-Dhikra al-thaniya ʿashara li-rahil al-katiba al-maghribiyya Malika Mustazraf], *Bayane al Yaoume*, September 14, 2018, http://bayanealyaoume. press.ma/الذكرى-الثانية-عشر ة-لرحيل-ةـالكاتبة-الم/.html.

20. *Wounds of the Soul and the Body* was published in 1999 by Editions Accent, a publisher that has since folded.

21. Moustadraf, interview by Ouafik, 2004.

22. Moustadraf, interview by Ouafik, 2004.

23. Moustadraf, interview by Ouafik, 2004.

24. Nasrallah, *Ayyami maʿ Malika* [My days with Malika], 116.

25. Moustadraf, interview by Ouafik, 2004. Moustadraf also wrote a searing indictment of the Moroccan health-care system's failures, and the lack of a serious activist response to the situation, in a nonfiction piece entitled "Those flaky, fakey, eighth of March women." The article was published on March 8, 2006 by the website Douroub, no longer in existence, which had been an early champion of her work. It's interesting to note the intensity of the specific scorn provoked in Moustadraf by a token show of solidarity with kidney patients, undertaken by a group of women in the name of International Women's Day. Hell hath no fury like a feminist failed by bourgeoise women. Unlike in her fiction, Moustadraf details the exact costs of a dialysis session here, and directly calls out the state for abandoning kidney patients and not keeping its promises. She refers to those who visit the hospital wards to offer support to the patients, without taking further action, as "morally bank-rupt." The full text is archived online, apparently since 2018. Malika Moustadraf, "Those flaky, fakey, eighth of March women" [Malika Mustazraf - Nisaʾ al-thamin

min maris al-muzayyifat.. al-muflisat], *Alantologia* (blog), accessed October 26, 2021, https://alantologia.com/blogs/13306/.

26. The full text of Bouzfour's speech appears in this article: Yassin Adnan, "Bouzfour's refusal of the Moroccan Writers' Prize provokes cultural debate and reaction" [Rafd Buzfur li-jaʾizat al-Maghrib li-l-kuttab yuthir radd faʿl wa-sijalan thaqafiyyan], *al-Hayat*, February 12, 2004, archived at https://www.sauress.com/alhayat/31195543.

27. The 2004 interview with Mouna Ouafik I frequently quote in this piece was apparently the reason Moustadraf's case came to the attention of the Saudi media, after it was widely shared. Upon her death, the newspaper published in full her overwhelmed letter of thanks to the editors, in an article with no byline: "Al-Riyadh stood by her in her treatment: death comes for Moroccan novelist Malika Moustadraf" [Al-Riyad waqafat maʿha fi ʿilajiha: al-Mawt yughayyib al-riwaʾiyya al-Maghribiyya Malika Mustazraf], *al-Riyadh*, issue 13958, September 11, 2006, http://www.alriyadh.com/185800.

28. Moustadraf, interview by Ouafik, 2004.

29. The Quran, a new translation by Tarif Khalidi, Penguin Classics, London, 2008.

30. Sahih al-Bukhari 5065: Book 67, Hadith 3, translation my own, based on https://sunnah.com/bukhari/67.

31. Moustadraf, interview by Ouafik, 2004.

GLOSSARY

Afarit (singular ifrit): Demonic supernatural beings, able to possess humans. Unlike the djinns (see entry below), these spirits are never good news and are strongly associated with the underworld.

Ah wa nos, bos bos bos: The chorus of the 2004 hit pop song "Ah wa nos" by the Lebanese superstar Nancy Ajram. Ajram often sings in the Egyptian dialect, as she does here, this snippet of the lyrics meaning "Yes and a half, look, look, look." At the time this story was written, Ajram's hits and the Coca-Cola ads featuring her would have been ubiquitous TV fodder across the arabophone world.

ʿAntar (Antarah ibn Shaddad al-Absi): A sixth-century Arab knight and poet whose name is a vernacular byword for "heroism," "chivalry," and "strength."

Aseria: From the word "asr," which means "afternoon," and is also used to denote the afternoon prayer in Islam. "Aseria" refers to the late afternoon time, after the prayer, when women working at home have a chance to take a break after a long day of housework and cooking to catch up with one another over tea or coffee and snacks, before duties recommence with the husband's return home.

Bouchaib El Bidaoui: A very famous Moroccan singer of the 1950s and 1960s. Assigned male at birth, El Bidaoui dressed in female clothes and sang women's songs in what sounded like a woman's voice.

Boughattat: A legendary being of the night, a scary ghoul who preys on the sleeping. Nightmares are said to be caused by Boughattat strangling the dreamer.

Bouhiouf: Used to denote a specific famine in Morocco from 1944 to 1945 that was caused by a combination of drought and French colonial policy on food distribution. The term may also refer to any famine caused by drought (such as during the 1980s, when people had to resort to eating wild animals and weeds). It has also become a term used to describe someone who is so hungry that they eat indiscriminately or insatiably.

Bouya Omar: A marabout strongly associated in Moroccan popular culture with curing mental illness, including lovesickness, which is traditionally seen as possession by djinns. Sufferers would go to Bouya Omar's tomb shrine to get their demons exorcised and be cured. This could involve being chained up inside the shrine for long periods of time. After years of ongoing accusations of human rights violation at the shrine—the existence of which was seen to reflect something of a mental health treatment vacuum—it was eventually shut down by the Islamic PJD administration.

Briwat: Triangular fried pastries, usually stuffed with chicken, minced meat, fish, or prawns, commonly sold as street food.

Casa brand cigarettes: An unfiltered and very strong brand of Moroccan cigarettes, cheaper than any other brand. In popular culture the Casa brand is associated with grit and chaabi culture. In the 1970s, it was a popular brand among student Marxists, Leninists, and unionists, who associated the more expensive, filtered brands with the bourgeoisie. By portraying a woman smoking Casa brand in "A Woman in Love, a Woman Defeated," Moustadraf implies her character's immense strength and fearlessness.

Chaabi: "Popular," as in "of the people." This word can have a range of meanings including "folkloric," "working class," "subaltern," and "resilient." Chaabi music covers a wide range of homegrown Moroccan styles and subgenres.

Cheikhas: Female chaabi singers known for their fierce and intense performances. These women are emblematic to some extent of the rebel woman who frees herself from the constraints of patriarchal society and becomes involved in political life.

Derija (also spelled as Darija): The main spoken language in Morocco. Its roots are in the autochthonous Moroccan language Tamazight (also known as Berber) and Modern Standard Arabic, and it has also incorporated elements of French, Spanish, and Latin. There are diverse regional varieties of the language across Morocco.

Djinn: Supernatural beings able to affect the mental and physical health of humans; they can be benevolent but are often associated with curses and bad luck.

Doukkala: A region associated in the urban imagination with parochialism, rugged living conditions, and bumpkins. In "Woman: A Djellaba and a Packet of Milk," the main character's father seems to have a superiority complex about being more civilized than his rural counterparts.

Faneed al-makana: Tiny, rock-hard, multicolored children's candy beads threaded on elastic or string.

Fatiha: The opening surah of the Quran (literally "the Opener") recited as a blessing in various contexts. Fatiha is also a woman's name.

Fteeha: The Derija version of the classical Arabic woman's name Fatiha, and a profane way to say "the opener" for a mundane context, in a non-Quranic way. Unlike Miftaha, the name doesn't have the connotation of an easily lost key to a tin of fish.

Gnawa: Gnawa musicians are healers, griots, medicine men, trance workers, and exorcists. When they conduct a ritual ceremony, a feast is usually part of the fee.

Green and blue banknotes: Fifty-dirham notes (each worth about five dollars) are green and two-hundred-dirham notes are blue.

Grima: Derived from the French word "agrément," a grima is an authorization to operate a mode of public transport such as a taxi or bus, granted by the state to people with certain needs as a source of income. In popular vernacular, it implies a stable source of income and therefore a state of self-sufficiency.

Gueddid: Dried, cured meat made from ribs and tripe.

Harcha: A kind of unleavened bread made from cornmeal and milk.

Izaar: A simple, single-sheet garment wrapped around the lower body. An izaar also serves as a bridal sheet.

Jabaan kul obaan: A garish multicolored candy shaped like a giant pole; pieces are cut off to be sold to children outside schools and at fairs and amusement parks.

Jihaaz: The bride price provided by the groom's family traditionally has two parts: the maher, which is mainly money, and the jihaaz, which consists of furniture and other items needed to equip the marital home (such as fabric, makeup, perfume, fruit, sugar, tea, and meat) and everything the bride needs for the hammam ritual (such as henna, toiletries, and jewelry).

Karian: Areas of unregulated urban development improvised by and for socioeconomically disadvantaged people, often migrants from rural areas. "Karian" is a specific Casablanca term, as it is a creolization of the French word "carrière," meaning "quarry." The first such residential area in

Casablanca was created by workers in a cement factory in the quarry next to their workplace, hence the name, which was then used for all such areas in the city. All the common English terms used to denote these types of residential areas are problematic, so I chose to retain the Casablanca Derija word.

Kawalib: A traditional solid-sugar phallic object used in a wedding ritual. The bride steps over the kawalib seven times in order to guarantee a healthy marital sex life.

Lalla Mira: A legendary Moroccan female witch figure associated with sexuality, and also seen as a water spirit. Known as a dangerous sexual predator to be feared, she is also loved and venerated and credited with great good by many people.

Sebsi: A clay pipe bowl on a long, thin wooden stem used to smoke kif, a traditional mix of finely chopped marijuana and indigenous tobacco.

Sirwal: A traditional type of pants or underwear worn in many parts of the world with a very baggy crotch almost down to the knees.

Slakeet: From the Arabic plural of "Sloughi," a type of sighthound dog endemic to Morocco also known as a Berber Greyhound. Since these dogs are commonly hungry strays, they are known for hanging around the streets hoping for food. When used in reference to a person, as here, it would be a complex word to translate, since it was originally used in a similar way to English terms such as "tramps," "hobos," "down-and-outs," but nowadays denotes the bored, unemployed young men who hang around on street corners. This disenfranchised community is seen as constantly getting in trouble, getting high, and hassling passing women.

Soussi faqih: In Islam, a faqih is a religious scholar. A Soussi is someone from Sous, a region of Morocco known for the depth and rigor of the religious and scientific education offered to students in centuries-old specialist schools there. In the context of witchcraft and possession, faqihs are thought to have sufficient knowledge and power needed to oust the worst demons, and those from Sous are considered the most knowledgeable and powerful of all faqihs.

Al-Habib, one of the famous Soussi faqihs teaching and practicing today, is said to control seven kingdoms of djinn. The current king of Morocco wears a tiny black bracelet said to have been made by al-Habib, presumably as a means of protection. So when the family of the suffering patient in "Blood Feast" call in a Soussi faqih, they are pulling out the big guns.

Thiqaaf: A black magic practice that specifically targets men's sexual ability. Typically, a talisman is sealed inside a matchbox and buried somewhere, activating a curse that will stop the target from ever getting another erection.

Toukal: Derived from the Arabic verb root أكل [a-k-l] meaning "to eat," toukal is a curse specifically linked to food and poisoning. Toukal is often said to be the cause of digestive problems and the sudden onset of conditions such as hepatitis and kidney failure.

Zoroastrians: Adherents of the religion Zoroastrianism (also known as Mazdayasna), one of the world's oldest continuously practiced religions. The religion is believed to have bequeathed monotheism, messianism, and concepts such as heaven and hell to various newer religions such as Christianity and Islam. Although Zoroastrianism places equal sacred importance on water as it does on fire, the religion is widely known for its fire temples and Zoroastrians are thought of as fire worshippers. In the vernacular used by the angry father in "Just Different," it's a shorthand for pre-Islamic heathenism and therefore a strong insult.

TRANSLATOR'S ACKNOWLEDGMENTS

In Malika's absence from this earthly plane, I have been blessed with the friendship, support, and wisdom of a brilliant community in Casablanca, Marrakech, and Rabat, without whom this translation would never have happened. I want to extend my eternal and basically boundless gratitude to my collaborator on various projects, my dear friend Noureddine Ezarraf, for diving deep into Malika's words and worlds with me in fascination, and teaching me so much along the way, as ever; to Aïcha El Beloui, who housed me, egged me on, made me laugh, kept me sane, and wondered at one point, "Are you planning to make a film of her life?"; to Sawsan Bourhil, who took me to Malika's café, tirelessly answered my questions about slang, and went in search of obscure details, in every sense; to Ruqaya Izzidien and Mosa'ab Elshamy, who made me feel like I was truly home; and to Mouna Ouafik, Abdelmajid Jahfa, Aida Nasrallah, Said Mountassib, Yassin Adnan, Ahmed Bouzfour, Zohra Ramij, Mehdi Annassi, Mehdi Azdem, George Trotter, and Soufiane Aboumalih for all of your different kinds of help and your great kindness along the way.

My immense love and gratitude to Iman and Ziko Hamam for hosting me and inspiring me during various phases of this book's development, and being part of all my work. For hosting and feeding me so well during the last weeks of putting this book together, Carlos Rubio and José Paleán, Lola and Julia Moron Vela, and Javi Ortigosa.

I'm truly grateful to Omar Berrada and Emma Ramadan for bringing Malika into my life in the first place. Thanks also to the enthusiastic commissioning editors of my earlier versions of some of these stories in English: Susan Harris, Jennifer Acker, Hisham Bustani, and Selma Debbagh; and to the team at Saqi London (especially Lynn Gaspard and Elizabeth Briggs) for creating a UK edition of this book.

And finally, deep and sincere thanks to the Feminist Press for becoming Malika's first real home in English, and to the whole team for working on this book so enthusiastically during the pandemic trauma. Before this book, I'd heard tell that Lauren Rosemary Hook was one of the best editors one could ever work with, and now I know it's true. May all writers everywhere be blessed with such profoundly co-creative and passionately committed editorial support.